A car squealed into the parking lot. Tyler took one look, and his blood ran cold.

The speeding car headed straight for Annie and Bethany, showing no hint of slowing down.

As its window rolled down, Tyler was running before the first shot blasted through the silence. Putting himself directly in front of his wife and daughter, he pushed them behind another vehicle. He covered them as well as he could with his body. Bethany's whimpered sobs broke his heart, but he made himself block them out.

More shots rang out around them. How many came from the marshals protecting them and how many from the people who wanted him dead, he had no idea.

* * *

AMISH WITNESS PROTECTION

Amish Hideout by Maggie K. Black–January 2019
Amish Safe House by Debby Giusti–February 2019
Amish Haven by Dana R. Lynn–March 2019

Dana R. Lynn grew up in Illinois. She met her husband at a wedding and told her parents she'd met the man she was going to marry. Nineteen months later, they were married. Today, they live in rural northwestern Pennsylvania with enough animals to start a petting zoo. In addition to writing, she works as a teacher for the deaf and hard of hearing and works in several ministries in her church.

Books by Dana R. Lynn

Love Inspired Suspense

Amish Witness Protection

Amish Haven

Amish Country Justice

Plain Target
Plain Retribution
Amish Christmas Abduction
Amish Country Ambush
Amish Christmas Emergency

Presumed Guilty
Interrupted Lullaby

Visit the Author Profile page at Harlequin.com.

Amish Haven

Dana R. Lynn

HARLEQUIN® LOVE INSPIRED® SUSPENSE

Special thanks and acknowledgment are given to Dana R. Lynn for her contribution to the Amish Witness Protection series.

Recycling programs
for this product may
not exist in your area.

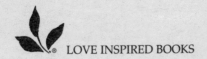

LOVE INSPIRED BOOKS

ISBN-13: 978-1-335-67881-2

Amish Haven

Copyright © 2019 by Harlequin Books S.A.

This edition published by arrangement with Love Inspired Books.

® and TM are trademarks of Love Inspired Books, used under license. Trademarks indicated with ® are registered in the United States Patent and Trademark Office, the Canadian Intellectual Property Office and in other countries.

www.Harlequin.com

Printed in U.S.A.

And now abideth faith, hope, charity, these three;
but the greatest of these is charity.
–1 Corinthians 13:13

To my family. Thank you for giving me the love and support I need to follow my dreams.

ONE

"You don't need to be concerned. I have it covered."

Tyler Everson heard his boss's voice as he walked past his office. He frowned. What was Gene doing here? Gene Landis, one of the most sought-after lawyers in the city of Chicago, had supposedly left three hours earlier to attend one of his wife's benefit dinners. He shrugged. It was none of his business. Tyler knew as well as anyone that law was a demanding career. Those who wanted to succeed had to be willing to make sacrifices.

He should know that. He'd lost his wife and child because of his job. Annabelle. He missed his wife still. And his sweet little Bethany. She'd be five by now. Did they ever miss him? A familiar ache spread through his chest. Unbidden, the memory of Annabelle leaving him came to mind. Her accusations of how he had become withdrawn and was no longer the man she had married echoed in the recesses of his mind. She was right, but not for the reasons she had thought. Tyler had wanted to run after her, to plead with her to stay. But he hadn't. Because due to his job, there was the possibility that she and Bethany could be put in danger. Tyler could never prove it, but he believed that her life had been threatened once before. There had been an accident that had left her with severe injuries. He had never believed it was an accident. Tyler had received threats after he had sent a man to prison for life. Threats that culminated in a runaway truck smashing into their home and injuring his wife. He still had nightmares about it. Annabelle had been horribly injured. Her legs had suffered extensive damage. Every time he had looked at the scars on them, he knew he had been to blame for not taking the threats seriously until it was too late.

She had been in the hospital while the police had investigated the incident. The police had looked into the threats, as well, but had been unable to find evidence against the man he suspected. In fact, they had concluded that the threats and the accident were unconnected. Annabelle had accepted their findings.

Tyler believed differently. Six months later,

the man who had threatened him died of a heart attack. He still couldn't get over his fear.

What if someone else came after him? He had made a lot of enemies on the job. Tyler knew that he couldn't allow his family to be in danger. And so, even though they lived only an hour away, he stayed away.

He shook his head, trying to clear the dark memories. They were better off without him. He couldn't change what had happened. Most days he worked so hard that he could barely think by the time he reached his apartment. And that was the way he preferred it. Otherwise, the memories of the family he'd lost would hound him.

He couldn't regret his decision, though. He knew that he'd done what he could to protect them.

No, it was better this way. How many people got the opportunity to be up for partner at a prestigious firm such as Landis Law at the age of twenty-nine?

Tyler continued to the parking garage, his mind full of the case he was preparing to prosecute. It would be a tricky one. Would the witness's testimony hold up? He had his doubts about the woman. She'd waffled on a couple of details. Part of him dreaded putting her on the stand. And not only because of her weak testimony. In his gut, he wondered if she was being honest. Having someone swear under oath was a serious thing—at least it was to him. His reputation depended on his providing credible witnesses.

Arriving at his car, he unlocked it and placed his briefcase on the passenger seat. Then he remembered the brief. He unlatched the black briefcase and searched through it. His heart sank. The brief he'd printed out to review that night before tomorrow's court case was still on his desk.

With a sigh, he shut the car door and jogged back to the elevator. It would only take five minutes to go and retrieve it, but he hated inefficiency. His schedule was too jam-packed for him to be wasting time.

Tyler returned to his office. There it was. He picked up the brief he'd printed out and flipped through it to make sure all the pages were present. If he had to come back for something else, he would not be pleased.

Finally, positive that he had everything, Tyler switched off his light and headed out again. Gene's light was on. That man worked even harder than Tyler did. He could hear the murmur of Gene's voice. He was probably on the phone.

I'll just stop in and remind him that I'm going directly to the courthouse tomorrow morning.

Sauntering to the open doorway, he popped his head in.

Crack!

Stunned, Tyler watched as his boss fell back in his chair, red blossoming like some obscene flower across the once pristine shirt he wore. Gene was still, his eyes staring vacantly. Was he dead? Tyler jerked his gaze to the man standing across from Gene. His back was to the doorway. But Tyler knew exactly who it was. He recognized the dragon tattoo rising up from the collar of his dark jacket. Wilson Barco. The most wanted man in town. The man suspected of running a crime syndicate that was involved in everything from money laundering and drug trafficking to murder.

He hadn't seen Tyler yet. That was the only thing that was keeping Tyler alive.

He had to get out of here. Backing away from the door slowly, Tyler moved as quietly as he could. It wasn't quiet enough. Spinning around, the killer snapped the gun up and aimed.

Tyler ran. The bullet meant for him smashed into the wall where he'd been standing. A watercolor painting crashed to the floor, glass skittering across the surface.

Tyler didn't give it a second glance. His only hope was to make it to his car. He kept his head low as he ducked around a corner. Another bullet, but this time it made a solid *thunk* as it was embedded into the wall. He bolted past the elevator. No way was he risking waiting for it to open. Even if he made it, he'd be a sitting duck once it arrived at the bottom. The stairs. No other choice.

Another gunshot. A hot pain shot up his arm. He'd been shot. Despite the pain, he kept running. A little pain was better than being dead. Which was what he'd be if he slowed down.

Darting through the empty lobby, he grabbed his lanyard with a shaking hand and swiped his badge in front of the security panel, unlocking the door to the stairwell. It beeped, and the light turned green. He yanked open the door and jumped through the entrance, pulling it shut as the killer burst into the lobby.

He hit the stairs as the next bullet pinged against the metal door. He didn't slow down. Even though the door automatically locked when it shut, he wasn't taking any chances. He had no idea how Barco had made it into the building after hours. For all he knew, he could have already figured out a way to by-pass the security system.

His feet made loud clanging noises as he rushed down the stairs to the basement. It couldn't be helped. He had just hit the second landing when he heard another set of shoes racing down the stairs behind him. He didn't have as much time as he'd hoped.

Reaching the bottom of the stairs, he whipped open the door to the parking garage and ran to where his four-door sedan was parked. It was still unlocked. Tyler hopped in and started the car, just as Barco burst out of the doorway.

Without fastening his seat belt, Tyler shifted into Drive and yanked on the gearshift harder than he had in years. The car jerked forward. Spinning the wheel, he drove toward the exit. His rear passenger window shattered. A second bullet hit the side of the car.

"God, help me!"

Tyler hadn't talked to God since his wife had packed up and left, taking their toddler daughter and his joy with him. He'd been so angry at God for not intervening. For not opening his eyes to what was happening. But even if God had shown him, would he have been able to change? He was a workaholic, just like his father had been. Plus, his work was his private mission. God hadn't helped him then, so he had decided he didn't need God.

He needed God now.

Tyler careened around the parking ramp leading to the exit. Glancing up into the rearview mirror, he sighed. The killer wasn't there. Yet.

The street was just ahead of him. All that separated him from the outside world and the parking garage was the long wooden gate arm. Out of habit, he slowed. The gate started to lift as the sticker on his windshield was registered. Another glance in his rearview mirror. His blood froze.

Barco was running up the ramp.

What was he doing? He stomped on the gas pedal. The engine roared, and the car shot forward. The boom barrier splintered as his car broke through it. He could hear an alarm sound as he pulled onto the street. The car he cut off braked and skidded, and the driver blared his horn at Tyler.

"Sorry, buddy," Tyler muttered.

Where did he go now? He had to go to the police. And then home.

Home. He couldn't go there. Barco had seen him pull out of his parking space. His very prominent parking space with his name on it. In this day of technology, it would be easy for anyone to find his identity and address. He had no doubt that if he went home tonight someone would be waiting for him.

He couldn't worry about that now. He had to go to the police. A vision of Gene flashed through his mind. What had he done to deserve being murdered?

He turned into the police station so fast that he barely missed sideswiping a police cruiser. He threw open his door and raced up the steps, holding on to his injured arm. The clerk at the window gaped at him for three seconds before rushing to assist him.

Two hours later, Tyler was sitting in a conference room at the police station. His arm had been cared for by the paramedics, and he'd been given something to take the edge off the pain. Fortunately, it wasn't a bad wound.

Officers had taken pictures of his arm and the side of his car. A team had been dispatched to the law firm. He'd heard something about an ambulance being sent there, as well. He remembered Gene's blank stare. He feared the ambulance was too late to do Gene any good.

An officer entered the room. Officer Cale. They'd worked together on cases before. Tyler had always liked the quiet officer. "Tyler, our men have caught Barco. They're bringing him in now. I hate to tell you this, but your boss—"

"He's dead." Tyler's voice was flat.

Cale nodded.

"Where did they catch Barco? Surely the man wasn't dumb enough to hang around the crime scene when you caught him."

Cale hesitated. Sensing more bad news, Tyler tensed.

"You were right that he would find out who you were. He was in your apartment."

Stunned, Tyler stared at him. Then some of the tension drained out of his shoulders.

"Good to know they caught him. Though I don't like that he was in my place." Tyler took a long drink of the bottled water they had brought him. He hadn't realized how thirsty he was.

Cale gave him a funny look.

"What?"

"You know it's not that easy, Tyler."

Before he had time to think about Cale's words, the door opened. A man who looked to be close to his age entered the room. Officer Cale straightened. The new arrival nodded at the officer before his gaze zeroed in on Tyler. His face was hard to read, but Tyler thought he could detect some sympathy in his eyes.

I'm not going to like this.

"Mr. Everson. I'm US Marshal Jonathan Mast."

Tyler's gut clenched. It couldn't be good if the US Marshals were getting involved.

"You're in a precarious position right now. Wilson Barco has his fingers in just about every crime venue you can imagine. But he could never be prosecuted because we could never find witnesses to his crimes."

Tyler nodded, not liking where this was going. He'd known that Barco had slipped through the cracks before.

"We believe that Gene Landis was on his payroll."

"No way. Not Gene!" He shook his head vehemently. Gene had always been a stickler about doing everything the proper way. And now to find out he'd been living a double life? He couldn't wrap his mind around it.

"Yes, Gene." Mast pulled out a chair and sat across from him. "Sorry, but that's what the evidence is adding up to. Barco is a man with vast resources. You are the first reliable witness we've ever had who could incriminate him. If we were to allow you to remain in your apartment, there's no doubt in my mind that you would be killed or simply vanish before you could testify."

For a moment, there was silence as Tyler thought through the matter. Finally, he spoke. "What's your plan? Will I get police protection? Go to a safe house?"

Mast shook his head. "Neither of those options would be enough. Barco's reach is too vast. No telling who we can trust. We're putting you in witness protection."

A sick feeling overwhelmed him. He knew all about witness protection. Those who went in lost all connection with their families. His daughter, Bethany—would he never see her again? Would she even know about him, or would she grow up and forget he even existed? And what about Annabelle? He had no hope of ever winning back his wife again, he knew that. He couldn't change who he was, and she had already shown that she couldn't accept that. Not to mention the danger he'd put her in if they were to get back together. But he'd never imagined a life where he could not even see her or hear her voice again.

The future that loomed ahead of him was dark and empty.

* * *

The hair on the back of Annabelle Everson's neck rose. Was she being watched? She glanced around the grocery store, but no one appeared to be paying any attention to them. She must have imagined it. She shivered, then blamed it on the air-conditioning.

Even though she knew it wasn't the cold that was making her shiver. This was the second time today she'd felt like someone was watching her. The first time had been outside the library, where she took her daughter every Wednesday afternoon for the reading hour. Today the library had been busier than normal. The local fire department had sent several of the firefighters and a truck to talk about fire safety. The children present were thrilled to get to touch a real fire truck.

After the library, she and Bethany went shopping. It was their weekly routine.

Annabelle pushed the cart down the aisle, listening as Bethany chattered on about the letter she'd received from her kindergarten teacher. Annabelle could hardly believe that her baby would be starting school in a month. Where had the time gone?

"Mommy, Tasha and Nikki said that their daddy is taking them swimming tomorrow."

Annabelle braced herself. Tasha and Nikki were the twins who lived two doors down from them. Since they had moved in three months ago, Bethany had started to talk about their daddy constantly. Which nearly always progressed to "Why doesn't my daddy do that?"

In truth, Annabelle wasn't even sure that Bethany remembered Tyler. It had been three years since she'd left him. He'd seen Bethany a few times after that, but not since she was three years old. She had seen pictures of him, though.

Her heart ached for her baby.

"Mommy, when will I see my daddy again?"

And there it was.

"Honey, I don't know. You know that. But I can take you swimming or to the playground with your friends if you want to go. I always do."

It didn't help. Bethany crossed her arms across her thin body and pushed out her lower lip. Oh, no. The last thing Annabelle wanted was for her daughter to go into a full meltdown in the middle of grocery store.

"Don't even think about throwing a tantrum, Bethany Jane. Or you won't be going swimming with your friends tomorrow."

Bethany glared, but wisely kept silent. Annabelle never proposed consequences she wasn't prepared to follow through on. It was one thing she'd learned as a single parent— something she'd never planned on being.

"Mommy, why is that man watching us?"

Forgetting her daughter's near tantrum, Annabelle swung her head in the direction that Bethany pointed. Her heart pounded at the thought that she'd finally see who was watching them. No one was. A young man in his early twenties was reading the label on a soup can. After a second, he dropped two cans into his shopping cart and moved past her to continue shopping.

"He's just shopping, Bethy. Like us." Despite her words, she couldn't relax. Her gut tightened. Her maternal instinct was on full alert. A mother knew when danger was near her child.

"Let's finish up and get home, okay? If we hurry, we can stop and get pizza for dinner."

Bethany's eyes lit up and she grinned. "Yay! Pizza! Can we get ice cream, too?"

Annabelle tousled her daughter's blond hair and smiled back. "Of course! What's pizza without ice cream for dessert?"

Happy again, Bethany skipped beside the shopping cart.

Annabelle hurried as much as she could.

She couldn't shake the thought that someone was watching again. She turned her head suddenly. Her eyes were pinned by the stare of the young man she'd seen earlier.

Bethany had been right. That was not the face of someone shopping. The cold stare she encountered made her shudder. All thoughts of shopping left her mind. She needed to get her daughter home, where they'd be safe.

"Bethy, come with me." Grabbing her daughter's hand, she abandoned the shopping cart and made for the exit. A glance over her shoulder confirmed her fear. The man was on his cell phone, watching her. She moved quicker.

"Mommy, what about the ice cream?"

"Honey, I will see if we can get it somewhere else. But we need to leave. Now."

Bethany was a very bright girl. She didn't argue with her mom. Looking down at her daughter, Annabelle could see that she was pale and her eyes were wide. She hated that her daughter was afraid. Better scared and safe. That was the important thing.

She tightened her grip on Bethany's hand and left the store. The little girl was trembling now. Who was that man? An image of him grabbing Bethany and running off flashed through her mind. Annabelle paused to lift her daughter in her arms. Bethany didn't question it but wrapped her legs around her waist while winding her arms around her mother's neck.

The parking lot was crowded. Annabelle ducked between two cars, crouching low. She set down Bethany, motioning her to keep low. Bethany squatted next to Annabelle. "Shh. Don't make a sound. Okay?" she whispered in Bethany's ear. The child nodded, burying her face in her mother's shoulder. Moving as if in slow motion, Annabelle raised herself enough to peer across the parking lot through the windows of the car on her left. The man was standing outside the store, talking on the phone while his eyes searched the parking lot.

For her.

What did he want?

Settling back down, she considered her options. Her car was three rows away. It would be practically impossible to get there without being seen. Or worse.

She peeked again. Oh, no. He was heading this way. Now what?

Putting her finger to her lips to let Bethany know to keep silent, she crouch-walked away from the row, heading toward the next one. Her daughter stayed close to her side. She glanced back. Not good. He'd seen them and was picking up his pace. His eyes were glued to her as he moved toward her.

"Run, Bethany!" Grabbing her daughter's hand, she ran as fast as she could with a five-year-old in tow. "Please, God. Keep us safe. Protect my baby."

A police car turned down her aisle and pulled in two cars away from her.'

"Thank You, Jesus!"

The officer stepped out of his car.

"Officer!" She ran up to the man. "Help! We're being followed!"

She pointed to the man who'd been following her. He was gone.

"Ma'am?"

She shuddered. "There was a man. He'd been following us around the store. When we left, he followed us out here. We hid, and tried to get to our car, but he saw us and was chasing us."

Her cheeks heated. The officer probably thought she was being paranoid.

"I was scared," Bethany offered in a shy whisper.

Fortunately, the officer seemed to believe them. "Ma'am, do you think you could give me a description of the man?"

An hour later, they arrived home. Bethany was happy. They'd stopped and picked up pizza and ice cream. Annabelle wanted to sleep for the next ten hours, she was so emotionally drained. Fear for her daughter still swirled in her head, but she wasn't panicking anymore. Going around the house, she locked and dead-bolted all the doors and windows. She was probably overreacting, but she didn't care. The whole situation had freaked her out.

She was cleaning up the dishes when her cell phone rang. She didn't recognize the number.

"Hello?"

"Annie, it's me." There was only one person in the world who called her Annie.

Tyler.

Her husband. The man she hadn't seen in two years.

"Annie? You there?"

She shook her head. "Yes, I'm here. It's been a frazzling day, Tyler. What do you want?"

A pause. "Something happened last night, Annie. I can't tell you everything, but the US Marshals are involved. I'm being put into witness protection."

"Witness protection?" Stunned, she lowered herself into a chair at the kitchen table. "Tyler, people in those programs have to completely disappear."

In her mind, she heard Bethany ask when she would see her daddy again.

"I know. It won't be forever. At least I hope it won't. I need to testify against someone. Maybe after that, I can go back to being me."

A sudden thought occurred to her. "Tyler, the reason you're going into witness protection… Would it affect me at all?"

"What do you mean?"

"Someone was following me today."

TWO

"Someone's following you?" Tyler exclaimed, horrified.

"Hey, don't shout at me!"

"Sorry." *Keep it together, Tyler.* "Where are you now?"

He heard an aggravated sigh. "I'm at home. I just put Bethany down to bed, and I'm exhausted."

She sounded irritated, but he hadn't lived with her for the first four of their seven years of marriage without learning something. She was frightened. She was covering it up, but he heard the tremble in her voice. Man, he hated that. She had always seemed so fearless.

"You never answered me. Could the man following me be related to what happened to you?"

That was a good question. He had the feeling she wasn't going to like the answer.

"I don't know. Annie, I will call you back."

He disconnected the call and went to the door of his room. He had no idea where he was. All he knew was that Marshal Mast and his team had hustled him out the back door of the police station the night before and driven for over an hour to this house.

An agent was coming down the hall. Tyler had met him briefly earlier. What was his name? Kurt? No. Karl. Karl Adams. That was it. "Could you tell me where I could find Marshal Mast?"

"Sure. Come with me."

Tyler walked beside the agent, his nerves on edge. What was happening at Annabelle's house right now? Was someone watching her? What about his daughter? Fear rose up inside him. How much danger was Bethany in? He was helpless to protect her, and it ate at him. He followed Karl Adams. A female agent with a tight dark bun smiled at them as they passed. He saw her gaze lingering on Karl. Karl left him at the office, then retreated to talk with the woman.

Marshal Mast was sitting at a laptop in an office at the back of the house. He glanced up from the screen as Tyler entered. Pushing back the headset, he allowed it to settle around his neck. "Something on your mind, Tyler?"

"Yes, Marshal Mast."

The marshal waved his hand. "We're going to be working together, Tyler. You need to get used to calling us by our first names. We don't want to announce to others that we're US marshals."

Tyler nodded. "Jonathan, then. I called my wife to tell her I was going into witness protection."

Jonathan frowned. Tyler had told the man that he and his wife were separated and wouldn't be getting back together. He could practically read the man's mind: *So why is he calling her?* He quickly headed off any questioning.

"She informed me that she and my daughter were being followed today."

At this information, Jonathan jumped to his feet. "Karl!"

Feet pounded in the hallway. Karl Adams entered the room at a brisk pace. "Jonathan? What did you need?"

Jonathan glanced up at Karl, a frown creating grooves in the flesh beside his mouth. "Karl, I need you to make a trip for me to pick up Tyler's wife and daughter. They may be in danger. Take Stacy with you. What's the address, Tyler?"

Tyler recited the address. Would Karl and

Stacy get there in time? How he wished he could go with them.

"Call her back, Tyler. Let her know he's coming."

She wouldn't be happy. Nevertheless, Tyler dialed the number. Annabelle answered on the first ring. He knew at once she was steamed.

"What's going on, Tyler? You call me out of the blue, tell me you're going into hiding, hang up on me and now you're calling me back? Do you know what time it is? What have you gotten yourself into?"

"Annie—"

He stopped. Jonathan held out his hand for the phone. Fine. Let him deal with her. She was too stubborn to listen to him, anyway. And too angry.

"Mrs. Everson? This is US Marshal Jonathan Mast. I am in charge of your husband's case. He tells me you thought someone was following you today?" He listened for a minute. It drove Tyler crazy not hearing her side of the conversation. What exactly had happened? Had it been an actual threat, or some freaky coincidence?

He didn't believe in coincidences. And he doubted that the marshals would buy that theory, either.

"Mrs. Everson, I need you to listen. I am sending a marshal to come get you and bring you to a safe house. Yes, it's necessary. I have every reason to believe that your life and the life of your daughter are in grave peril."

Grave peril. He'd failed his family again. Despite his best efforts, he'd brought danger to their door. If Annabelle was scared, his daughter was probably terrified.

The daughter that he hadn't seen in two years. Guilt swamped him. He knew why he'd made the choice not to be a part of her life. It had hurt more than anything he'd ever done to distance himself from his family, but he knew it had been for their own good. He was saving them from heartache and disappointment. And possibly from danger.

Except now he wasn't sure if he'd done the right thing, because danger had found them, anyway.

Jonathan got his attention when he set the phone back down.

"So, what's the plan?" Tyler asked. "You're going to protect them, right?"

"Let's bring them here first. Then we'll decide. I will do my best to see that you are all protected."

It was a long night, waiting for Annabelle and Bethany to arrive. His nerves were stretched tight as he paced through the house. He couldn't eat, and he was too wound-up to relax. He forced himself to try to sleep, but it was useless. In his mind, every possible scenario played out, each one worse than the one before. Finally, he gave up trying to sleep and decided to watch a movie to help pass the time.

It was a little after two in the morning when a car pulled up the lane. He shot to the window and peered out. Was that Karl? It was too dark to see, but who else would it be? The grating noise of the garage door opening seemed overly loud in the silent house. Jonathan walked out of the office.

A minute later, the door connecting the kitchen to the garage opened up. Stacy walked in, her dark brown hair starting to escape from the bun at the nape of her neck. She held the door open. Karl walked through the open door and flashed her a tired smile as he passed her. He was carrying a sleeping Bethany against his chest. Tyler was startled by the surge of jealousy that shot through him. That should have been him carrying her. Immediately, he felt ridiculous. The man was protecting his daughter, after all. He should feel grateful, not jealous.

His attention shifted to the woman who had entered behind Karl.

Annie.

Even exhausted and scared, she was beautiful. Her hair was shorter than it had been the last time he'd seen her, brushing her shoulders in straight waves. But it was still a lustrous deep brown with hints of red in it. And her eyes… He'd never forgotten those toffee-brown eyes. Eyes that were guarded as they met his.

He'd hurt her badly during their marriage. How could he expect her to understand, much less forgive him?

"Tyler." Just that one word, said in a voice devoid of emotion, told him that forgiveness wouldn't come easy. As she stepped farther into the room, she swayed once.

Jonathan moved forward. "Annabelle. We can talk in the morning. I have you and Bethany in a room in the back." He led them away, glancing back once at Tyler sympathetically.

Tyler was left standing alone. He was always alone.

But at least he could sleep now.

The next morning, Tyler was reunited with his daughter. Unlike her mother, Bethany was overjoyed to see her daddy. She was a little shy at first, hanging back. A tight sensation crept into his chest. She didn't know him. Why should she? After a few minutes, though, her natural curiosity and her happiness at seeing her father overruled her bashfulness. His heart melted as the bright child snuggled up to him and told him all about her two best friends, identical twins who lived down the street, and her excitement to begin kindergarten.

He glanced at Annabelle. She listened, her face strained. She didn't have to say that she wasn't pleased with the turn of events. It was clear on her face.

Karl Adams stepped into the kitchen, a fierce frown on his face. Stacy approached Tyler and attempted to persuade Bethany to leave Tyler's arms. No easy task. The child wanted to stay with her father. Eventually, the marshal succeeded. Holding Bethany's hand in hers, Stacy led her from the room. Her eyes met Karl's as she passed him. Something was going on with those two, but Tyler was too concerned about his daughter and Annie to give it much thought. Karl turned his eyes back to meet his. Tyler tensed.

As soon as the child was out of earshot,

Jonathan indicated that Karl should go ahead and speak.

"Jonathan, you were right. Barco has put a price on Everson's head. Every criminal within a hundred-mile radius will be gunning for him." Karl shifted, his gaze sweeping over Annabelle. "He's also offered money for Annabelle and the child. Probably to smoke Tyler out of hiding."

"Can't you stop it?" Annabelle blurted.

"No, ma'am. Barco has more resources at his disposal than we know about. He has managed to escape capture for years. Every potential witness has been compromised or disappeared. Evidence has disappeared. Plus, he's always managed to have an alibi. It's been impossible to prove his guilt. Until now. Which means he'll be pulling out all the stops to eliminate Tyler."

The ticking of the clock on the wall was unnaturally loud in the silence.

"What's going to happen to my daughter and me?"

The quiet whisper from his wife made his heart ache.

Karl answered. "You're in danger as a result of your association with Tyler. The US Marshals will help you go into the witness protection program, as well."

* * *

"No."

Any other time, the sight of all these big men sitting with their mouths open would have been amusing. Right now, she was just trying to keep herself from panicking. It took all her effort to keep the tremors that were making her stomach quake from showing up in her voice.

"Annie—"

"No, Tyler!" She swung back her gaze to her husband. He hadn't changed much since she'd seen him last. Still handsome. His brown hair was on the longish side, blue-gray eyes that reminded her of the ocean on a cloudy day, and that square jaw, now covered with several days' worth of whiskers. Once, he could persuade her to do anything. Not anymore. She was through letting him bother her. She was in charge of her life. It was by his own choice that he wasn't a part of their lives anymore. "I understand that you are in trouble, but that has nothing to do with me."

"Ma'am." One of the agents stepped forward. She was so upset, she couldn't remember the man's name. "It would be safer for you if you came with us."

"I'm not going into hiding. I can go on vacation for a bit with Bethany. Leave the area. Then when this all blows over, I can come back."

"I don't think—" the man began.

But she was done. "I don't care what you think. Tyler and I haven't lived together for three years. He hasn't been to see us, including his daughter, in over two. If anyone was searching for him, we wouldn't be the people to go to. I am not disrupting my life again for him. We'll go to my mother's house. She lives in Southern Illinois, five hours from where I live. My brother is a cop. He lives a little over ten minutes from her. He can protect us."

The marshals tried to convince her to change her mind. She wouldn't budge. Tyler tried to talk with her, too. Every time he moved toward her, she glared at him. Finally, he seemed to get the message. He wasn't happy about it, but she didn't care. He'd made his choice when he'd let them go. She quickly squelched any pity she might have felt for him.

They couldn't hold her against her will. She knew it, and they did, too. Nor could they force her to go into the witness protection program. That didn't stop them from giving her disapproving frowns. She ignored them all.

Strangely, while their frowns didn't bother

her, Tyler's silence did. The way his eyes followed Bethany around. He stuck close to his daughter.

Annabelle couldn't take it. If she didn't know better, she'd think he really was concerned. A sliver of guilt tried to wedge itself into her mind. Guilt that she was going to be separating a father from his daughter. Maybe forever. She shoved aside the guilt. She didn't have time for this.

She walked into the kitchen to demand that they either put her and Bethany in a taxi, or take them home.

She never got the words out.

Marshal Mast, who'd insisted she call him Jonathan, leaped to his feet as his phone went off. Not the phone he'd been talking on throughout the day. Annabelle figured that was his work phone. This one had to have been his personal phone. Especially since it was playing a popular song for the ringtone.

"Celeste?" he blurted into the phone.

She watched, amazed, as the calm US marshal paled. Her brow furrowed. Hopefully it wasn't too serious. Instinctively, she glanced at Tyler to see his reaction. His eyes were narrowed as he watched the marshal. Obviously, he had no clue what was going on, either.

That could have described their whole situation. It was surreal.

"Okay, honey, relax. Do what the paramedics tell you. I'll be there as soon as I can." Jonathan's finger trembled as he disconnected the call. "Karl, you're in charge. My wife just went into labor at the shopping mall. They are taking her to the hospital in an ambulance."

"She'll be okay, Jonathan." The female marshal she'd met earlier, Stacy, stepped forward. "We know what to do here."

He nodded, then rushed to the back of the house. Within minutes, he ran past them and out the front door. She heard his car start up and pull down the lane.

"Remember when Bethany was born?"

Annabelle jumped. When had Tyler moved up beside her? She had been so fascinated by the escaping marshal that she hadn't seen Tyler moving.

Memories of happier times flooded her brain. She smiled. "I thought I was going to have her in the car."

"Me, too! I was terrified. I'm still shocked I didn't get a speeding ticket."

She turned to face him. As she did so, she noticed for the first time the corner of a gauze bandage peeking out from the sleeve of his T-shirt. "What happened to your arm?"

He hesitated. "Wilson Barco shot me. While I was running from him."

Her blood ran cold. No way. She needed to get her daughter away from him. Even as she cringed at being so coldhearted, she hardened her resolve. She had to put Bethany first. There were some things her daughter shouldn't be exposed to. Bullets were one of them.

Something of what she was feeling must have shown on her face. Tyler hastened to explain. "It's not a bad wound. Seriously. I need to keep it clean for a few days, but it should heal fine."

She shook her head. "Tyler, I know what you're trying to do. And I'm not changing my mind. If someone doesn't drive me home, I'll call a cab. I'm sorry you're in this mess. I truly am. But it's your mess. And I don't want any part of it."

She turned her head away so she didn't see his reaction.

Karl Adams wasn't happy. "Look, Annabelle, if you won't go into the witness protection program, will you at least let us drive you to your mother's house? It would be safer than driving you to your own house."

Annabelle thought about it. What did she really need to get from her house? It would be nice to have her own car, but it wasn't worth their lives. Nor did they desperately need anything from inside the house. She already had some bags packed from when Karl and Stacy had picked them up.

"I will agree to that. A marshal may drive us to my mom's house."

Karl visibly relaxed at that. It was a safer and smarter decision, and she knew it.

In a remarkably short time, Annabelle and Bethany were in a car with a younger marshal, heading to her mother's house. Talk was scarce on the drive. Although the marshal, Rick, seemed like a nice man, Annabelle's stomach was in knots. What if she was making a mistake? She clenched her teeth, refusing to second-guess her resolve.

A couple of times, Rick tried to engage her in small talk. She did her best to answer but found herself distracted.

After an hour or so, she allowed herself to lean against the door and close her eyes. Every time she would begin to drift off, though, a noise or the motion of the car would jerk her awake, her pulse racing.

The third time it happened, Rick glanced at her out of the corner of his eye.

"Ma'am, it's not too late to turn back. We would keep you safe."

Shaking her head, she sat up.

"Thank you, Rick. I mean it. But I really think we'll be fine at my mother's house."

Even as she said it, Annabelle suppressed a shudder.

Recalling the events of the past two days, she wondered if she would forever be looking over her shoulder.

THREE

Exhausted was too weak a word to describe how Annabelle felt as Rick finally pulled into her mother's driveway Thursday evening.

Nerves had her continuously checking her side mirror to make sure that no one was following them. A couple of times, she got spooked by a car driving too close. Rick took no chances, to her relief. If he thought a car was suspicious, he would turn off the road, or see if it would pass them. Every time, the cars would pass them or keep going straight. It didn't help her relax. The danger was still very real.

When they were an hour away from her mother's house, Rick allowed her to call her mother on a burner phone.

"If they are tracking you, using your cell would be too dangerous."

Her mother didn't pick up. The answering machine kicked on. "Mom, are you there? Mom?"

"Annabelle? I didn't recognize the number."

"I know. Listen, I'm going to be at your house in an hour. A friend is driving me."

The last hour of the trip dragged on and on.

Her mother was up waiting for them. Annabelle had told her as much as she dared on the phone. She didn't mention Tyler. Even if she wasn't going into witness protection, he was. It wasn't a good idea to broadcast that information, even to her mother. Instead, she told her that someone had been bothering them at home and she needed a safe spot for a few days, so that she could figure out her next move.

Rick waited until she was inside before he left.

"Thanks, Mom." Annabelle leaned into her mother's arms as she stepped through the door. Bethany hovered at her side, blue eyes bleary with sleep.

Nancy Schmidt kissed her daughter's cheek. "You know you're always welcome, sweetheart." She turned to her granddaughter. "Bethany, do you have a hug for your grammy?"

Bethany lifted her arms to her grandmother, yawning as the woman pulled her close. "Tired, Grammy."

"You should have invited your friend in for a few minutes." Curiosity burned in Nancy's eyes.

"He couldn't stay," Annabelle replied, not meeting her mother's eyes. Thankfully, the older woman allowed the subject to drop.

"Have you eaten?"

Annabelle and Bethany both shook their heads.

Nancy bustled them toward the kitchen. "I heated up some mac-'n'-cheese. Eat, then you can go to bed. We can talk in the morning."

A gentle sigh slid from Annabelle. She should have known that her mother would have something ready for them to eat, no matter what time they showed up.

Forty-five minutes later, Annabelle was in her old bedroom, staring into the darkness. Her mind wouldn't settle down. Had she made the right decision? At the time, she'd been so angry, so scared. Now? Now she was worried that she might have brought danger to her mother's doorstep.

Maybe the people after Tyler would leave her alone once he disappeared.

Or maybe they'd become more aggressive.

Lord, grant me wisdom. Help me to do the right thing and protect my little girl.

Around midnight, she finally dropped off into a fitful sleep. Her rest was interrupted by nightmares. Nightmares of a stranger taking Bethany. She ran after him, but he kept running. Just when she thought she'd catch him, he'd vanish right in front of her. Bethany was crying out for her to save her, but she was always too far away.

Bolting straight up into a sitting position, Annabelle panted like she'd been running, sweat clinging to her skin. The sun was just starting to peek through the windows. It was early. No other sounds stirred in the house. She slipped out of the bed, welcoming the familiar comfort of the shag carpet under her bare feet. She could do with more sleep, but the thought of returning to bed made her shudder. Instead, she headed toward the shower.

When she emerged, she followed the aroma of fresh coffee and cinnamon rolls to the kitchen. Her mother was awake, but Bethany was still in bed. Poor thing, she had to be wiped out after all they'd been through in the past couple of days.

"Hey, Mom." Annabelle helped herself to a cup of coffee, added some mocha creamer, then slid into a chair at the table.

"Annabelle." Nancy scooped a warm cinnamon roll onto a plate and placed it in front of her daughter with a fork. "I would ask if you slept well, but I can see you didn't."

Annabelle sighed. While she considered what to say, she forked a bite of the pastry into her mouth, closing her eyes to savor the sticky-sweet flavor. "Mmm. Delicious. I had trouble sleeping. Too many things happening." She raised her eyes to her mother's concerned face. "I keep worrying if I should have come here. I hate to think I put you in any kind of jam."

Her mother clucked her tongue. "Now, don't you be worrying about me. You and my granddaughter are my priority. Always have been."

"I know, Mom. I just—" She broke off as her cell phone rang. Tensing, she looked down at the number. "Hold on, Mom. It's Danielle, a woman on my block. Bethy was supposed to go swimming with her daughters yesterday."

She didn't comment on the obvious reasons why they hadn't.

She tapped the screen to answer and took a deep breath. "Danielle? What's up?"

"Annabelle, are you and Bethany okay?" Danielle's normally peppy voice was nervous.

How to answer that? *Oh, yeah. Just being followed. Oh, and my estranged husband is going into hiding after seeing his boss get killed. Not.*

Trying to be upbeat, she said, "We're fine. On a little trip, that's all. Why? Is something wrong?"

A slight pause. When Danielle's voice came again, it was softer, like she didn't want anyone to hear her. "Listen. I don't want the girls to worry, but something weird is going on. Mike said there was a car parked across the street from your house yesterday morning. And someone was sitting inside it. There's no house across the street from you, so why was he there? Mike was walking the dog at lunch and they went right past the car. Mike thought he had surprised the guy. He wasn't positive, but it looked like the man was looking at your house through binoculars."

A shiver worked its way up Annabelle's spine. Danielle might not have been sure, but she had no doubt Mike was right. They were waiting for her.

What would have happened if she had gone home first, the way she had planned?

"Thanks, Danielle. I will call the police. I appreciate your letting me know."

"There's more." Of course there was. "Yesterday afternoon, someone was going around the block with a picture of you and Bethany.

He was insisting that he was your cousin and trying to reach you on urgent business."

Her stomach turning, Annabelle closed her eyes.

She didn't have any cousins. Where did the man get the pictures?

Annabelle couldn't get off the phone fast enough. As soon as she hung up, she dialed Tyler's number.

"The number you have reached is no longer in service." She wanted to cry at the automated message. Tyler's phone must have been disconnected so he could disappear. Now what?

Wait a minute. Karl Adams had given her his card.

Jumping to her feet, she ran back to her bedroom to grab her purse. This was not a conversation she wanted her mother to hear. Shutting the door, she began rifling around her purse frantically. After a few seconds, she found the item she was looking for.

Her fingers shook as she tapped his number into her smartphone. When Karl answered, she breathlessly repeated her conversation with Danielle Johnson.

"Hold on, Annabelle. I will call you back as soon as I know something."

He hung up quickly. Sinking down on the

edge of her bed, Annabelle fought to control her emotions. The urge to cry battled with the urge to throw something. She did neither. Instead, she sat tensely, clasping her phone between her hands like a lifeline. *Please, Lord*, she repeated over and over and over in her mind.

She checked on Bethany. She wasn't awake yet, which gave her a little more time. Returning to her bedroom, Annabelle paced as she waited. Every minute or so, she looked at the screen on her phone to see the time.

When her phone rang forty minutes later, she nearly dropped it.

"Y-yes?" she gasped.

"Annabelle? You were right to call. I sent someone to your house. It's been ransacked. I have the feeling that the pictures that man was showing your neighbors were from your wall. There were several empty picture frames on the floor, and it was obvious pictures had been taken from the walls. No doubt someone was trying to find something that would lead them to you. The problem is, there are bound to be many people after you because of the bounty put on your head. Who knows how many people are watching your house. Whatever you do, don't leave your mother's house.

And stay inside. The last thing we want is for you to be recognized."

"I won't! Oh, I'm just so scared right now. What if my mom's in danger because of me?" She shouldn't have come. Oh, why had she been so stubborn?

"I understand your concerns. We're coming to get you. What?" the marshal said to someone on his end. "Here."

A moment later, Tyler came on the phone. "Annabelle, can you convince your mom to go stay with your brother for a while?"

She nodded. Oh, wait. He couldn't see her. "Yeah, I think I can do that. I'll see if she can stay at Ethan's place."

"Do it. She'll be safer at Ethan's house."

"Tyler—"

He was no longer on the phone. "Karl Adams again, ma'am. Someone's on the way. I agree with Tyler. Your mom needs to get out of the house. We'll see that she's safe. But you and your daughter need to go into hiding. They won't stop coming for you."

Six hours later, she and Bethany were led into a house in Iowa. She'd never been to Iowa before. Now that she was here, though, she had zero interest in looking around at the scenery. Guilt over the disruption to her mother's life weighed heavy on her. Inside the house, Karl was there. And so was Tyler.

"Daddy!" Bethany ran to her father, throwing herself into his arms as if she hadn't just seen him for the first time in years a little over a day ago. Her sweet daughter apparently harbored no bitterness toward the man who'd always chosen business over family.

She couldn't be so blasé. The bitterness she'd shoved deep down inside, for her little girl's sake, erupted.

"What are you doing here?"

Tyler blinked. "What do you mean? I'm going into witness protection, just like you."

A familiar tall woman stood up from the table. For a brief moment, Annabelle paused, trying to recall the woman's name. Ah. Stacy Preston. That was it. Stacy smiled at her and intervened in what promised to be a heated reunion. "Why don't I take Bethany to see if we can find something fun to play." She gave Karl a meaningful look.

"Excellent idea, Stacy."

She wasn't sure, but Annabelle thought she saw the man wink at his colleague. As she watched, the very efficient female marshal blushed and ducked her head.

Annabelle waited until Stacy left the room with Bethany chattering beside her, then turned to her husband again. "You and I are both going into witness protection. But we are not going together. It's your fault we're even in this mess."

Tyler felt as if he'd been punched in the stomach. Her words knocked the wind right out of him. Not that he could deny her accusations. He couldn't. It was all his fault. While he might not have asked for any of it to happen, he had once again brought danger to his family.

But this time, he wasn't going to walk away.

"I can see you are put into separate placements," Karl began slowly.

Uh-uh. No way.

"Could we have a moment, please?" Tyler shoved his hands deep into his pockets. He needed to convince Annabelle of his sincerity.

A slight smile touched the marshal's mouth. "Of course. There's a small dinette off the kitchen. Why don't you go in there? I'll make sure you aren't disturbed."

Tyler motioned for Annabelle to precede him. She crossed her arms in front of herself and glared. "Please?"

Huffing, she tossed her brown hair over

her shoulder and marched in the direction the
marshal had indicated. When they arrived in
the room, she didn't sit, but faced him. Her
chin raised a notch, as if she was daring him
to speak. If the situation hadn't been so serious, he might have been tempted to smile.
She was as adorable as he'd remembered. As
it was, there was little cause for humor. Their
very lives were being ripped apart.

"Annie—" he began.

"Annabelle," she interrupted. "No one calls
me Annie. Not anymore."

"Fine, Annabelle. Look, I know I screwed
up. I put my work ahead of you and Bethany.
I left you alone when I should have been with
you. I made it impossible for you to stay. I
get that. And I know I don't deserve a second chance."

"You're right." Her nostrils flared. "Do you
know how many times she's asked for you
these past two years? Of course you don't!
Because you weren't there. But I'm used to
that. Even when we were together, you were
never there. And now you show up again, but
only because you've dragged yourself, and us,
into danger. It infuriates me knowing that it
took someone gunning for you to bring you
into your daughter's life. And what happens
when this is over? You disappear again?"

Annabelle stepped closer to him. He could almost feel the energy of her anger crackling off her skin. Her rich brown eyes shimmered with her rage. "She was too young to remember being abandoned before. If you distanced yourself again, it would wound her deeply. I have to protect her from that."

Would it wound Annabelle, too? He knocked that thought out of his head. He had no right to expect to be welcomed back into Annabelle's life. They were strangers now. But his daughter… He couldn't bear the idea that she would grow up and not know him.

"I wouldn't abandon her."

Annabelle snorted, cutting her eyes at him. Her scorn made him wince.

"I'm serious. Annie… Annabelle." Tyler ran his hands through his hair and breathed in deeply. He needed to think. To make her see reason. "There's no way to tell how long this case could drag out. It could be months. It could be years. None of us would be safe until it's over. If we go into separate placements, I would never see my daughter again. Please, Annabelle. This is my last chance to be a father to her. I don't want to disappear on her again."

He could see her jaw tensing. She didn't immediately say no. A bubble of hope swelled in his heart. For the second time in less than a week, he turned to God and pleaded for help and guidance.

"I need to think." Annabelle walked out of the room, without giving him another glance. His heart sank.

A minute later, Karl appeared in the doorway. "Well?"

Tyler sighed. "She needs to think. I can't blame her."

"We can't let her think too long. I'm sorry, Tyler, but time is something we just don't have."

Right. Tyler hadn't felt this helpless in a long time.

"Karl!" Rick, another marshal, rushed into the room. "You need to see this."

"Coming now, Rick." Karl nodded once at Tyler, then left the room.

Once again, Tyler was alone with his thoughts. He was tempted to go after Annabelle again and try to reason with her, but really, what was the point? She'd obviously made up her mind. And he couldn't say he blamed her.

If only she knew about the reason he'd pushed her away. How it had been for her safety. Somehow, knowing that she was in danger even though he'd kept away from her made his reasoning back then seem ridiculous.

A sudden flurry of action caught his attention. Karl marched out to the garage, his phone to his ear as he barked out questions. His intense expression didn't bode well for the current situation.

Karl called a meeting with Tyler and Annabelle. A couple of other marshals were in the room. He could hear Bethany squeal with laughter in the other room, where she was playing. A smile spread across his face at the sound. When he considered that he might never hear that joyful sound again, his chest grew tight. Rubbing his chest, he turned his head to find his wife staring at him, frowning slightly, her head tilted like she was trying to solve a puzzle.

A throat cleared. Tyler reluctantly removed his gaze from Annabelle and turned it on Karl. He didn't like the look in the marshal's eyes. Karl was worried about something, and the way the man continued to watch him told Tyler he strongly figured in whatever was on Karl's mind.

"Tyler, there's been a complication," Karl said finally, confirming his fears. "Jonathan had planned to place you in Colorado. He had a job lined up for you and your new identity was in the works, but we have to change our plans. It seems that Wilson Barco has doubled the bounty on your head. There have already been reports of men resembling you being attacked in ten states, including Colorado."

Annabelle gasped, her eyes showing her shock. "So what does that mean? What happens now?" Annabelle's voice was quiet. He knew that voice well. It sounded calm, but it really signaled that her emotions were spiraling very close to the surface.

Karl turned to her, his expression smooth.

"It's not unexpected," Karl told the group. "We have been monitoring the airways and computers for anything. An undercover contact has informed us that the bounty has stirred up interest in several states. Plus, Barco has apparently called in favors from all over the country. There's no way for us to know all the people who are out to get to you. We're working on a different placement right now. One that will take you farther off the grid and out of Barco's reach."

Tyler felt as though he was sinking in quicksand. He had heard much about Wilson Barco during his time as a prosecuting attorney. The amount of power the man wielded was terrifying.

Was there any place they could go that he wouldn't find them?

FOUR

Off the grid?

Annabelle stared at the marshal, appalled. What exactly did Karl have in mind when he said "off the grid"? Mentally, she envisioned them living in a rustic shack in the middle of the woods. *Little House on the Prairie*–style. She quelled a shiver of distaste. She was not a woman who enjoyed camping. Too many creepy crawly things. If it wasn't for the danger to her daughter, she'd back out now. However, since her daughter's life was at stake, she held her silence. There was nothing she would not endure to protect Bethany.

She regretted thinking that she would be able to protect her little girl without the protection of the marshals.

"Annabelle?"

She turned her head and met Tyler's eyes. The concern in them was clear. "I just want to go back to a normal life and forget that all this happened, Tyler. I want to wake up in the morning and know that Bethany is safe. Instead, I know that from this point on, I am going to be constantly looking over my shoulder. I hate that."

"Annie—" Tyler began. He broke off when Stacy entered the room. Without Bethany.

"Where's my daughter?" Annabelle winced at the harsh note in her voice. She'd always thought of herself as someone who could keep calm in an emergency. This whole experience was testing that theory.

Stacy, fortunately, seemed to understand. She flashed a sympathetic smile at the nervous parents. "She's fine. Really. She fell asleep while I was reading to her. I'm guessing she was pretty worn out from the past couple of days."

Annabelle felt a small niggle of guilt. Her baby girl was suffering because of her stubbornness. If she had just given in gracefully when the situation had first come up…

No! That was not productive. She had been doing her best to protect her child. That was never the wrong thing to do. Now she was starting to second-guess her choices, and she wasn't going to go down that road. She had second-guessed herself for months after she left Tyler, but when he never made any effort to get her back, she realized that she had been right.

She'd also realized that she hadn't wanted to be right. Not that time.

The conversation drifted into more logistics. She doubted that she'd be able to add anything. Solitude. That's what she needed. Just a few minutes to herself, so she could think.

Pushing her seat back, she stood. Immediately, all conversation stopped and the marshals and Tyler all focused on her.

"Is it all right if I excuse myself for a bit?" She wasn't really asking but thought she should be polite. Out of the corner of her eye, she caught the small grin that crossed Tyler's face. Ah, apparently, he was on to her.

"Of course!" Karl stood, deep furrows digging into his forehead. "Are you all right? Anything we can do for you?"

She felt ridiculous.

"Relax, guys. She just needs some time to herself to process. She'll be fine."

Annabelle felt her jaw drop as she turned to look at Tyler. She was amazed that he had realized that about her. Granted, they had been married. But it had seemed back then that his attention was always on other things. She'd often wondered if he was truly listening to what she had been saying.

He had just proven that he had been. She wasn't sure what to think about that. And that scared her. Because she needed to keep up her guard around him. She had given him her heart once, and he hadn't appreciated it, choosing his job over her and their daughter. She couldn't allow herself to make that mistake again.

It was getting hard to breathe in the room, being so close to him.

She walked into the living room area to check on Bethany. The blanket from the couch was on the floor. Bethany, however, was not on the couch. Annabelle frowned. She had thought that Stacy had left her in the living room, but maybe she had put her in one of the bedrooms.

Stomach flipping like she had swallowed a couple of frogs, Annabelle ran to the first bedroom and opened the door. Her heart raced as her fear spiked. She had to swallow past the scream that had lodged in her throat. Spinning around, she checked each bedroom. They were all empty. Where was her baby?

She wasn't going to stand here, though. She had a house full of US marshals to help her. And Tyler.

Running back through the house, she burst into the room. "Bethany's gone!"

Tyler jumped to his feet so fast that his chair tipped over. No one even glanced at it.

"I'll check the rest of the house!" Stacy charged off. Annabelle could hear her feet pounding down the hallway.

"The rest of you, check the perimeter. Rick, check the garage. If she's not there, join us outside."

Without another word, the search began. Annabelle ran outside after Karl. When he turned to her, she shook her head. "Don't you dare tell me it's safer inside. No one is going to keep me from searching for my daughter."

Wisely, the lawman let the subject drop.

The group spread out. Within a few minutes, Stacy and Rick had rejoined them and were helping to comb the yard for Bethany. Annabelle had barely held back a sob when she had told them. She had been holding on to the hope that Bethany was playing in the house and she just hadn't seen her. Now that hope was gone.

The air was suddenly split by a child's shout.

"No! I want my mommy!"

Bethany.

"Quiet, kid." The cold voice sent ice through her veins.

"No! Let me go! Let me—"

Annabelle's knees turned to water as her daughter's shout was suddenly cut off. She couldn't allow herself to falter, though. Her baby needed her. Karl waved his gun in the air, indicating that they should follow him. He pointed at Rick and signaled something. Without breaking stride, Rick turned the corner and disappeared on the other side of the house.

She understood. They were going to try and box in the villain who was taking her daughter. What if they were too late? "Hurry," she whispered.

A hand touched her back. She didn't scream. She knew that touch. Tyler was right behind her. For some odd reason, his familiar touch was comforting. She drew in a deep breath as they continued to follow Karl around the side of the house. He was moving so slowly. Even though she knew in her heart they had to move with care, she found herself practically stepping on the heels of the marshal's black shoes.

As they turned the corner, her horrified eyes met with a sight that would haunt her for the rest of her life. A young man in his twenties was dragging her struggling five-year-old daughter across the lawn. Bethany was small, but she was also wiggly. And she was putting all that wiggle to good use now. The man was having trouble keeping hold of him.

"Halt!" Karl bellowed, snapping his gun up.

Annabelle clutched the man at her side. Dimly she was aware it was Tyler, but she couldn't help herself. What if he shot and hit Bethany? It took all her will not to say something. She had to trust that he knew what he was doing. It was the hardest thing she had ever had to do. So hard, she tasted blood from biting her lip in her agony. Needing to be strong, she released Tyler. She swayed briefly, but his hand touched her on her back and steadied her.

The young man did halt. He swiveled, putting himself behind Bethany. He strapped the young girl against him with a muscular arm and yanked a knife out of his pocket. Instead of showing fear, a sneer slipped onto his face.

"You ain't gonna shoot me. 'Cause if you do, you might hit the kid. She's my insurance. There's a lot of money riding on me bringing her daddy in. And unless you let us go, and he comes with me, then she might get hurt. It's that simple."

"Please." Was that strangled voice hers? Annabelle swallowed the fear that clogged her throat. "Please. She's just a little girl."

He laughed. She shuddered at the sound. Stacy placed a hand on her shoulder. She had been so wrapped up in the scene playing out before her that she hadn't realized the marshal was beside her.

"Now, bring her daddy out to me."

Wait. What? She glanced over her shoulder, where her estranged husband had been standing mere seconds ago. There was no one there now. Her heart chilled in her chest. Had he abandoned them, right when they needed him?

No, she couldn't believe that. Yes, he had chosen work and his life over them before. But she had seen the caring in his eyes when he interacted with his daughter.

But she couldn't deny what her eyes were telling her.

Tyler was gone.

There was no way he was going to let that man hurt his daughter.

Tyler crept back into the shadows and stole up behind the man holding the knife. He saw a thick branch, about a foot long, and grabbed it. Stepping carefully, he concentrated on making a minimum amount of noise as his feet inched closer to his goal. It was a good thing it was summer. The lush green grass cushioned his steps and softened any noises. He could clearly make out the man's voice through the shrubbery. And he could hear the pleading voice of his wife.

He winced, remembering the man who'd promised to hurt his family years ago. He had hoped that when he had disappeared from their lives, they would be safe. And yet, they were once again at the mercy of a madman. But this time, he refused to sit back and let the criminals chase him away while those he loved were hurt. He would gladly sacrifice himself if it meant that Bethany and Annabelle would be well and protected.

But the world didn't work that way. Danger was everywhere.

He could see the man's head now. The man still held the knife. It wasn't touching Bethany. In fact, the knife was being held almost six inches away from her. Finally, something was going his way.

Glancing over, he knew the moment that Annabelle became aware of his presence. Her eyes widened slightly. Quickly, she jerked away her gaze. She again began to plead with the man. *Good girl.* Tyler knew that she was distracting the punk so he could act.

Karl was glaring. It was hard to tell if his hard stare was aimed at Tyler or at the criminal, but he would guess that the glare was pointed to him. He didn't have time to care. Not when his daughter was in trouble.

The young man was growing angry. "Stop your crying, lady! I want you to go get this kid's dad or there's going to be trouble."

Tyler took the final two steps forward. "I'm right here."

The villain jerked around in shock. Bethany wiggled from his loosened grasp and ran to her mother's arms. Annabelle took her daughter in her arms. Immediately, Stacy stepped in front of mother and child, shielding them from harm. Tyler saw Karl glance their way. His gaze locked on Stacy for a moment. It might have been his imagination, but Tyler was certain that fear lurked in Karl's eyes at the sight of the female marshal in the line of danger.

The man with the knife glared in Annabelle's direction. There was nothing he could do. Bethany was firmly out of his range. Fury crossed the man's face. Raising his knife, he charged at Tyler.

A shot cracked out. Howling, the man

dropped his knife from his bleeding hand. He didn't pause long. Tyler was ready for him. The moment he started forward again, Tyler swung his branch like a club. The man went down, stunned.

Within seconds, the marshals swarmed over him and had him restrained. Karl pulled the phone out of his pocket and demanded extra marshals at the house. Tyler heard him say something about the safe house being compromised. Duh.

"What were you thinking, Tyler?" Karl growled. The cords on his neck were strained. He was probably fighting not to holler.

"I was thinking that I needed to save my daughter."

Karl didn't say anything as the dazed would-be kidnapper was loaded into the back of Rick's car. In silence, the group watched Rick bend his tall frame down to get behind the wheel and drive off.

"Annabelle, let's take her inside." Stacy gathered Annabelle and Bethany and herded them toward the house. Tyler watched them go. Seeing them safe was worth any chastising he might receive from Karl. Before she disappeared from his view, Annabelle threw a look over her shoulder at him. Gratitude shone in her eyes. Tyler stood taller. Karl might have thought he acted rashly, and perhaps he had. But his wife appreciated what he had done.

The moment the women were gone, Karl turned back to him.

He was in for it now.

"Tyler. Man, I don't even know what to say. What you did? It was all kinds of stupid. You could have gotten hurt. Bethany could have gotten hurt. It—"

"You watch your daughter being kidnapped and tell me that you wouldn't try to save her." Tyler tightened his jaw. The memory of that dude dragging his daughter away made his blood boil again.

Karl sighed, running his hand through his hair. "Look. I understand why you did it. I do. I get it. But, Tyler, that could have gone seriously wrong. You have to let us do our jobs."

Tyler didn't say anything. What was there to say? He couldn't promise not to act if his daughter, or if Annabelle, was in danger again. Shaking his head, Karl sighed.

"Come on, Tyler. We need to get inside and get mobilized. Obviously this safe house is no longer safe. We'll have to find a new place to hide you and your family until the details are final."

Tyler and Karl reentered the house. Soon

after, new marshals and the state police were patrolling the perimeter. No chances were being taken with the safety of his family. He did appreciate the effort they were going to for them. The marshals went into action and searched for evidence that the house had been bugged. They checked every room, the cars, even the cell phones. Nothing.

He just had to stay alive until he could testify. Would the threat disappear then? Barco seemed to have so many resources, Tyler wasn't sure if he could ever return to normal society.

What would he do if, even after today, Annabelle decided to go into the program separately? He would have no more chances if she did that. He rubbed his chest, trying to soothe the ache that had formed. Karl disappeared into his office, his phone once again at his ear. Tyler sat by himself for the next half hour, trying to get a handle on his emotions.

He stood when Karl emerged from the office. The marshal strode with purpose down the hall. Curious, Tyler followed.

Karl marched into the kitchen. Annabelle was sitting at the table with Bethany and Stacy. The marshal motioned for her to come. Warily, she stood and went with him. Karl led them into the office. When they entered, he turned and shut the door behind them. Gesturing to the chairs in front of the desk, he seated himself behind it. Tyler had no idea what he was going to say. But he braced himself for the worst.

"Did Bethany say what happened, how he got to her?"

Annabelle bit her lip. He had to look away momentarily. He couldn't be distracted by her right now. "She said she woke up and heard a dog barking outside. Bethany has been wanting a dog for a long time. When she went out the back door, she couldn't find a dog. She found a man who tried to coax her into his car." Annabelle threw a haunted look at Tyler. His gut clenched. "She knows she's not supposed to talk to strangers. When she turned to go back inside, he grabbed her."

Tyler shuddered as the reality of how close they had come to losing their daughter rippled through his mind. Too close. They needed to go into hiding as soon as possible. Whatever wiggle room they'd had, it was gone now.

Karl seemed to be on the same page. He turned a grave expression toward Annabelle.

"Annabelle. You have to decide what you want to do," Karl stated. "We are running out of time. Once you are placed, you will have no further contact with anyone from your past or from your current life. Not friends or coworkers. Not even your family. That's the only way that I can protect you. Do you still want a separate placement? I can find you one. That wouldn't be a problem. However, if you decide that you do still want that, it means after today, you and Tyler will have no more contact with each other until the threat against you ends."

"If it ever ends." Tyler hadn't meant to voice the thought. But now it was hanging in the air between them. Karl acknowledged the truth of the statement with a nod.

"Unfortunately, there is that possibility."

Tyler held his breath. He couldn't believe how much it hurt to have it spelled out that way.

The marshal wasn't finished. "Or, I can place you together. If you want, I can even place you for a short trial period. If it doesn't work out, we can consider a new placement. Whatever you decide, I will do. But you have to decide now."

Annabelle dropped her head. From where he sat, Tyler could see her clasp her hands together tightly. The knuckles whitened. Finally, she lifted her head and leveled her stare at Tyler.

"I am so angry with you, Tyler Everson." His heart sank. She was going to ask to be placed separately. He was going to lose his daughter. "But even though I am angry, it would be wrong for me to deny you your daughter. If I was positive you didn't care for her, I wouldn't hesitate. I think you do care, though. Especially after seeing you trying to save her."

Annabelle switched her gaze to the marshal. "I will agree to our being placed together." She held up her hand to stop them from speaking. Like he would. His emotions were too high. "I don't want to commit. I will agree to go on a trial period."

Karl stood. "Excellent. I need to make some calls. Get everything set up. Everything should move fast from here on out."

"Do you have any thoughts as to where you'll put us?" Tyler stood. Visions of a cramped apartment or a small house in mainstream suburbia rolled through his mind.

"I know exactly where I'm placing you. You'll be going somewhere no one would ever think to look for a high-powered lawyer and his family."

That was good, right? Just what they wanted.

"Where?" Annabelle asked.

Karl Adams smiled. "You're going to be living with the Amish."

FIVE

"Do you know where you're going?"

Annabelle shut her eyes and squeezed the bridge of her nose with her fingers. She had tossed and turned all night. Saturday morning had dawned bright and clear, in direct opposition to her mood. It was agony listening to her mother's tearful voice quavering over the phone. As much as she wished she could comfort her mother, she knew there was nothing she could say to make the situation more acceptable.

"I'm sorry, Mom. Karl didn't say where we were going. And even if he did, you know I can't tell you any of that."

She flinched as her mother sniffed. This was so hard. Tyler had taken Bethany to another room with Stacy to keep the fractious child occupied while she said goodbye to her mother. Possibly forever. It hurt so much to think about that. She had gotten used to talking with her mother every day on the phone. Or Skyping with her mom and Bethany. How was she supposed to not talk with her at all? How would her mother handle it? Ethan wasn't married, so Bethany was her only grandchild. The woman doted on her.

"It's cruel. Can't the marshals protect you from here?"

That worried her. She knew her mother. The woman was independent to a fault. She hadn't been happy about moving in with her son, no matter how temporary a situation it was. "Mom, you're not staying in your house, are you? I thought you were planning on going to stay with Ethan for a little while."

Her mother hesitated. "Well, I don't know, honey. I am used to my own ways. Besides, I have been in this house since before you were born."

Uneasy, Annabelle held the phone tighter, as if she could force her mother to see reason. "Mom, you have to go. Please. I would be constantly worried about you if I thought that you weren't safe."

She heard a muffled conversation. Then Ethan's voice came on the line.

"Hey, little sis. Don't you worry about Mom. She's stubborn, but so am I." That was true. When they were children, Ethan's stubborn nature had caused them to butt heads more than once. As an adult, however, his stubbornness had transformed into a determination that had served him well in his capacity as a lawman who was sworn to serve and protect. He would never let his mother remain in danger. He would use every argument he could to get her to agree to go stay with him.

She huffed a laugh, some of her tension draining. "So you'll make her go to your house?"

"Yeah. You don't need to be concerned about that. She might not be happy, but she won't want you to worry, so she'll do it."

That was probably true.

Tears again clogged her throat. "Oh, Ethan, I'm going to miss you guys so much."

His voice was slightly unsteady as he answered. "None of that. We'll miss you, too, but we will see each other again soon. Mom and I will be lifting you guys up every day in prayer." He paused. "Are you sure you want to go into hiding with Tyler, Annabelle? He isn't exactly the most trustworthy guy."

She bit her lip. She knew what Ethan's opinion of her husband was. She'd used Ethan's shoulder to cry on too many times for him not to be skeptical now. "I do. It'll be okay. He's changed. I can't really describe it, but I think this is the right decision. And I want Bethany to have a chance to know her father."

"Hmm."

Clearly, he didn't share her confidence. But she was sure that the change she had seen in Tyler was real.

She let the silence dangle between them, unsure of what to say to ease her brother's mind. What could she say? The situation was deplorable. A man had murdered someone, and Tyler had seen it happen. Now that man was willing do anything to make sure Tyler couldn't testify.

Including harming a five-year-old child.

That, more than anything else, was the deciding factor for her. She couldn't stay when her baby was in danger.

She hung up with her family, feeling alone. This was going to be the hardest thing she'd done since the day she'd walked out on Tyler. He had changed so much since they had gotten married. Missed important events, including her father's funeral. And he had gotten so withdrawn, she felt she was sharing her house with a stranger. Tyler had even stopped communicating with her. They would go through an entire evening without talking.

But she had still loved him. Had ached for

the man she had married to return. But she could not continue to live in a house filled with such tension and silence. She had grown up with a distant workaholic father. The toll it had taken on her mother was painful to watch. She refused to be that woman.

She now knew that deep inside, she'd hoped that her leaving would have been a wake-up call to him and that he would have come after them. When that hadn't happened, she'd been devastated. Thankfully, she had Bethany to be strong for. And she had her mother's shoulder to cry on.

Now, however, she was going into the unknown. What did she really know about the Amish? She'd seen them, sure. The women always wore dresses and they had white bonnet-type hats on. And they didn't use electricity or drive cars. That was the extent of her real knowledge. She'd never actually met anyone who was Amish.

Looking down at her jeans and sneakers, Annabelle frowned. She'd have to wear a dress. All the time. She hadn't worn a dress in years. She even wore dress slacks to church. Skirts would allow the horrible scars—scars that she kept hidden at all times—on her legs to show. Part of her had always wondered if Tyler had been repulsed by them. It was after the accident when he had started to really withdraw. What other reason could there have been for the change in his behavior?

And now she was going to be wearing a dress. Would the scars show? She tried to remember how long the dresses worn by Amish were.

Feeling slightly panicky, she wished the marshals had let her keep her cell phone so she could search the internet to research Amish clothing. She thought back to the Amish women she had seen in Indiana once. She recalled the women wearing dresses that were calf-length or longer. And most of them wore black stockings, too. So, even if she was forced to wear a dress, her scars would remain hidden. Cautiously, she inched her jeans up above her ankles and a couple of inches up her calves, about the length she thought an Amish dress might be. She twisted to the side to try and see if her scars peeked out below the denim hem.

"Annie? Are you ready to go?" Tyler walked around the corner.

She looked up at him guiltily, letting her jeans drop back down. They were all waiting for her, and here she was wasting good time. Where was her good sense? Not to mention her common courtesy!

Had he seen what she doing?

His face was softer than normal. She flushed. He knew what she was doing.

Only Tyler knew how much the scars bothered her. Only he would understand why she was looking up Amish dresses. A strange look crossed his face. Was it guilt? He looked almost haunted. But that didn't make any sense. The expression was gone so fast, she wondered if she was misreading him. After all, it had been several years since she'd last seen him.

"No one will see them, Annie," he said softly, almost whispering. "Even if they did, you have nothing to be ashamed of."

She shrugged, her cheeks still warm with embarrassment. "Why would I feel ashamed?" She hedged. "These scars are old news. I should be grateful that I survived the accident. Not worried about some scars."

Pain flashed in his face, although she had no idea why. He opened his mouth. Shut it. Paused. Finally, he sighed. "It's time to go. Have you done everything you needed to here?"

"Yes-s-s." She dragged out the word, disturbed by his attitude. Tyler had been going to say something different. She knew it. But she wasn't sure she even wanted to know what it was.

She needed to be careful. Being in his company again was affecting her more than it should. Oh, she was still angry at him. She wasn't sure if she could ever forgive him for giving up on her so quickly. For putting work and money ahead of her and their child. But seeing him now, watching him risk himself for Bethany, well, it softened the edge of her anger. If she wasn't careful, she was worried that she'd become emotionally involved again. She couldn't afford to do that.

Turning from him, she picked up her and Bethany's suitcases. All of the worldly possessions they'd be bringing into their new life were in the two red cases. Her lips twisted. She could probably leave most of the clothes behind. After all, once they arrived at the place Karl was taking them, they wouldn't be needing them.

Tyler couldn't get the image of Annabelle's face as she looked at her scarred legs out of his mind. She still harbored insecurities about her scars. Tyler wanted to tell Annie the truth—the accident had been a deliberate act of malice, and a warning. A direct result of his job.

Tyler had always believed that it was a warning for him. The runaway truck that had smashed into their front window and pinned his wife to the wall a week after he'd been threatened by the son of a man he'd sent to prison was too much of a coincidence.

Unfortunately, that man had an airtight alibi for the time of the accident. Tyler had understood the message. His family would suffer, just as the guilty man's family was suffering. Tyler had been in torment about what to do for weeks. Until the man had died unexpectedly and he could breathe again.

Eventually, the thought that he needed to save his family from himself had grown in his mind. When Annie had left him soon after, he'd taken it as a sign that he needed to let them go. Only then could he be sure they would be safe. And only then could he freely work to prove what the police had been unable to. It was a task he'd only recently been able to do.

The idea of telling Annie the truth crept into his mind. He scoffed at the idea. Yeah, right. Tell her that it was his fault she carried the scars, inside and out, that still bothered her. He finally had a chance to be with his daughter. He knew that he had destroyed all his chances to have a relationship with Annie. But he could still be a father to Bethany.

A few days ago, he didn't even have that.

"Let's move out," Karl ordered.

Rick slid behind the wheel of the car taking Tyler and his family. Tyler hadn't had a chance to speak with the man since he'd returned the night before from hauling Bethany's would-be kidnapper to the proper authorities. He wanted to ask him if the man had said anything more, but that would have to wait.

Karl led the way in his car. Stacy brought up the rear. The convoy was made less obvious by the fact that the cars were all different. Rick was driving a dark-colored SUV. Karl was in a midsize pickup truck and Stacy followed behind in a Jeep. Tyler sat in the front seat, next to Rick. Annie sat behind the driver's seat, and Bethany was securely fastened into her booster seat behind him. Tyler opened the mirror on his visor to look back at his daughter.

"You doing okay, bug?"

The smile she shot his way warmed his heart. "Yeah, Daddy. This is fun! Isn't it, Mommy?"

Annabelle rolled her eyes. "Absolutely. A blast."

Rick chuckled. Tyler winked at his daughter in the mirror. She was precious.

Rick's phone rang. He frowned when he glanced at it. Tyler went on full alert. "Something wrong?"

"Huh?" Rick checked the mirror, then switched lanes, following Karl. "No, not really. This girl I dated a couple of times, she keeps calling me. I am not sure why. We went out to a movie and to dinner. I told her that I would be busy with work for the near future."

Annabelle made a face behind him. Uh-oh. He knew what she was thinking about. When they'd still been together, he'd often been too busy with work to do things with his family. Even before he'd withdrawn.

"As long as we're okay."

"Yeah, I think we're fine. It'll probably be a boring trip. Sorry, but this isn't a very exciting drive."

Tyler settled down to enjoy the peace of the drive. It was a warm day outside. As the day heated up, Rick turned the air conditioner on higher. Around noon, Bethany started to whine about needing to use the bathroom.

Rick called Karl and told him that they needed a restroom break.

Tyler turned around partially in his seat. "We're gonna look for a place to stop, bug, okay?"

The smile she had given him earlier was gone, replaced by a definite pout. "Wanna stop now. I don't like this car ride anymore, Daddy."

"Bethany Jane," Annabelle said, her tone a clear warning.

"Two named. That sounds serious," Rick murmured. Tyler held back a grin. He knew Annie's tone all too well. It wouldn't go well if she thought he found his daughter's attitude entertaining.

Bethany gave up her whining, although her pout became more pronounced. Tyler winced, wondering how long they would have to wait for a full-out meltdown. The kid had had a rough couple of days. She was about due for one. Not that it would be acceptable. But it would be understandable.

Ten minutes later, they pulled off the interstate and headed for a rest area. Bethany nearly leaped out of the car when he opened her door. Even Annie groaned as she exited the vehicle and stretched. She caught him watching her and grimaced.

"You okay?" He stepped closer to her.

"Fine." She waved her hand dismissively. "Just ready to get there. Wherever there is."

That, he understood.

"Mommy!"

"Okay." She reached out for her daughter's hand and threw a tired smile at the men. "We'll be right back." Stacy joined them, and the three females headed off together.

Karl walked over to where Tyler and Rick were standing. "We should be there in about four hours."

Tyler groaned. Four more hours in the car. They had a portable DVD player. He'd gladly listen to kid videos if it meant his daughter would be entertained.

"Here come the women," Karl said, halting his discussion with Rick.

Tyler turned to see Stacy leading the way back, followed by Annabelle and a much happier Bethany skipping at her side. He heard a heavy sigh behind him. Glancing over his shoulder, he was astonished to see the wistful expression on Karl's face as he watched the women. Eyebrows rising, he slid his gaze back toward them. Stacy's eyes skittered away from the men, her cheeks flushed. He tightened his lips so he wouldn't smile. They might think they were playing it cool, but anyone with eyes could see that there was something going on between those two. He shot a glance over at Rick and snickered as the marshal rolled his eyes. Yep. They weren't fooling anyone.

Absently, he rubbed his arm where he had been shot. The bandage was off now, although his arm was still tender. He thought about his relationship with Annabelle. He missed the way they used to be so close. Shaking his head, he closed down that line of thinking. He shouldn't waste time on what was. What they had was gone. They were not going to be together forever. Only until they could leave witness protection. Then they'd go back to their separate lives. Although, this time, he would keep in touch with his daughter.

A car squealed into the parking lot. Tyler took one look and his blood ran cold. The speeding car headed straight for them, showing no hint of slowing down. When the window rolled down, he was running before the first shot blasted through the silence.

"Get down!" he yelled at Bethany and Annie. Behind him, Karl echoed the command.

Tyler reached the women and put himself directly in front of his wife and daughter. He pushed them behind another vehicle. He felt Annie flinch when the car door was hit. He pushed Bethany's head down and covered them as well as he could with his body. Bethany's whimpered sobs broke his heart, but he made himself block them out.

More shots rang out around them. How many came from the marshals and how many from the people who wanted him dead, he had no idea. Stacy landed beside them, her Glock in her hands. Her pretty face was drawn and serious. She was every inch a US marshal, protecting those in her charge.

"If we could get you into my Jeep, we might be able to escape while Rick and Karl are keeping them busy. I have called in the state police. They are on their way."

She led the way to her car, motioning for them to keep low.

Tyler put Annie in front of him and sandwiched Bethany between them. Slowly, they crawled to the Jeep. Another shot rang out and this time, it was accompanied by a loud cry. They had almost reached the Jeep when it was hit. Twice. Both rear tires hissed as the air left them. They weren't going anywhere fast in a vehicle with two tires deflated.

"You guys have to get to shelter." Stacy kept her eyes firmly on her targets as she spoke to them.

Tyler swiveled his head from side to side, searching for a safer place.

"Let's head to the trees. Run!" Tyler scooped up his daughter in his arms and ran, keeping Annie in front of him.

They had almost reached the trees when he heard a shout. Instinctively, he slowed and looked back. Karl was squared off against the villains, who had spotted them. One of them started up toward them. Stacy stepped behind a tree for cover and held her Glock in front of her. "Keep going," she ordered them. "I will hold them off. The police should be here soon. Then I or Karl will come and find you."

Tyler opened his mouth.

"Move, now! I need to focus."

Tyler turned and pushed his family behind the trees. He managed to glance back over his shoulder. Karl and Stacy were standing near each other, doing their best to keep the bad guys at bay. Rick was standing to their left, his face grim in his determination.

As he watched, Rick tumbled to the ground, his hands clutching his side. From where he stood, Tyler could see blood seeping between his fingers and covering his hands. His mouth went dry. A gasp at his side reminded him of Annabelle and Bethany. He needed to get his family to safety.

SIX

"Do you think Rick is dead?"

Tyler sighed at Annie's softly spoken comment. He had wondered how much she had seen. If she hadn't seen Rick go down, he had every intention of telling her, once Bethany was not paying attention. He just knew that there were some things one couldn't unsee.

"I don't think he was dead." He flicked his gaze toward Bethany. Good. She didn't appear to be paying attention to them. "He was still moving. I have no idea how badly he was hurt, though. I imagine that the police will be there soon, and they'll call an ambulance." He glanced behind him. No sign of Stacy. Or Karl. Where were they? Were they safe?

He winced at the sorrow on Annabelle's face. The urge to put his arm around her, to comfort her, was strong. But he knew that she wouldn't accept comfort from him. He was fortunate that she was talking to him. He could expect nothing more than that, though.

"I think we need to keep going, Annie. I wish we still had our cell phones. We could try and contact them later."

"I still have Karl's card," Annie murmured. "Maybe we could find a business that would let us use their phone."

He pursed his lips, considering. It was a good idea. "I think that would work. If we can't reach them, we could contact Jonathan Mast. Although I would hate to disturb him right now."

She thought about it for a few seconds, then nodded. "Sounds like a plan. Which direction do we head?"

"We're close to La Porte, Indiana. At least, I think we are. I seem to recall signs for I-80. We would have taken that next. I am guessing that we want to keep heading east toward Ohio."

"Mommy, I'm hungry."

They exchanged glances. The food was back in the car. "I have a protein bar in my purse, baby doll. That will have to do for now."

It wasn't the best choice for a five-year-old, but it was better than nothing. Especially since they had no idea how far they would have to walk before this adventure came to a conclusion. Annie opened her mouth to say something—he had no idea what—when he heard something. Holding a finger to his mouth, he listened. Annie froze, then she bent down and whispered to Bethany to be very quiet. His heart ached when his baby girl opened her eyes wide, her lower lip trembling. The poor little girl had been through enough that she realized they were not playing a game.

"Mommy, I'm scared."

His throat tightened.

"It's going to be okay, sweet pea," Annie whispered back. "Daddy knows what to do."

He did? That was sure news to him. Right now he was winging it. But he would do whatever he needed to if it would keep them safe.

Another patch of white noise. Followed by a burst of speaking. Like a pager.

Or a walkie-talkie.

They were being tracked through the woods. For a moment, he hoped that they were being tracked by the cops or the marshals. If so they would be safe for the time being.

"We have tracks in the dirt here," an unfamiliar masculine voice said. The white noise followed.

"Go ahead and shoot on sight. If you can

catch the kid or the woman, they can be used as bait."

Nope, definitely not the cops. He looked down at the ground, and irritation with himself grew inside. They were leaving all kinds of tracks in the dirt, scuffing up the path. That would never do. He leaned closer to Annie, so he could whisper in her ear. The scent of her hair threatened to distract him, but he refused to allow that to happen.

"We need to get off the path. Head into the brush and try to keep from leaving clear tracks." His old Boy Scout motto of Leave No Trace came to mind.

Annie nodded. Tugging gently on Bethany's hand, she indicated which way they were going. Thankfully, his daughter seemed to grasp the urgency of the situation. She followed her mother's lead without question. It was another plus that they'd all worn jeans that day. Otherwise, their legs would have been scratched up from the shrubbery. A couple of times, thorns caught at his ankles.

Without pausing, he bent over and picked up his daughter. "So she doesn't get stuck with thorns," he murmured in response to Annie's raised eyebrow.

She nodded and kept going. The voices were coming closer. Though they were still on the path. There was no way that they could get far enough away to safely avoid them, judging by the pace with which the voices were catching up to them.

Tyler stopped and glanced around. A little farther on, there were two trees that had been toppled. There was an opening between them. If they could squeeze down in there, maybe they could get low enough that they wouldn't be seen as the men went past.

"This way!"

Moving as quickly as the prickly bushes and briars would allow, the small group slogged through the growth and arrived at the tree.

"Let's get you in there first, and then I will lift Bethany to you." Tyler assisted his wife over the first tree. It was enormous. When he handed his daughter over to her mother, Annie set the child down. The top of her head barely cleared the tree. Perfect.

Placing a hand on the top of the fallen tree, he vaulted over and landed with a slight *plop* next to them. Annie had already coaxed Bethany to crouch down. He got down as low as he could. In the close confines, he could hear them breathing. He placed his hand on Annie's shoulder to urge her to crouch lower. His hand tingled where he touched her. She flushed. Did she feel it? He removed his hand and focused on listening.

"Lord, protect us." Annie's whispered prayer resonated within him. When was the last time he prayed, really prayed? Would God even hear him now, after he'd ignored Him for so long? He had nothing to lose. And he and his family could use all the help they could get.

God, please be with us. Keep us safe. Amen.

It was all he could think of to say. Hopefully, it would be enough.

By now, the men were practically on top of them. Their voices were growing louder. Even a bit angry. It suddenly struck Tyler that they were making no attempt at all to keep quiet as they tracked his family. Were they so confident in their ability to catch Tyler that they didn't put any effort into sneaking up on him? Could they really be that arrogant?

"Jim, they had to have left the path," one of the men said.

Jim. He now knew that one of them was named Jim. He would, of course, relate that to the police or the marshals. Not that it would make much of a difference. Jim was a very common name.

"Cut through here."

Lowering himself farther, Tyler put an arm across Bethany's shoulders, just in case she decided to stand for some reason. He didn't think she would, but she was only five. She whimpered softly in his ear. He tightened his arms around her.

"Steady, bug," he breathed. "I've got you." He placed his lips against his baby girl's soft blond curls. Over her head, he met Annie's wide eyes. She was frightened, but she was strong. He had always known that.

Then the men were right over them. If one of the men glanced down and to the side in just the right way, there was the chance that they would be seen. And there was no way to escape from their present hiding place. Had he put them in an impossible situation?

Another prayer whispered through his brain. *Distract them, Lord. Please draw them away from us.* Something crashed in the underbrush on the other side of the path.

"That way!"

He held his breath as the men dashed off, their voices loud and surly as they continued the search in the opposite direction. Tyler and Annie remained still and kept Bethany quiet for an additional ten minutes.

When it seemed that the men were gone, the tired group rose again. Tyler assisted Annie over the tree, then handed Bethany to her mother. When he had joined them, they started off again.

"I don't wanna do this anymore," Bethany whined. "I want to go home."

"Bethany, we are going on a little adventure, honey. I need you to be my brave girl for a little while longer."

How Annie could turn this horrific experience into an adventure was just part of what made her so amazing. However, the child wasn't buying it. Her bottom lip pushed out and her thin arms crossed her chest. He might not have been around her much, but he knew stubbornness when he saw it.

So did Annie. She glanced at him. He shrugged, as if to say, "Don't look at me, I got nothing."

"Bethany," Annie said, "I know that you're tired. I know that you are hungry. But there are bad men who are after us. We need to keep going so that they won't catch us."

That pushed-out lip started to tremble again. "But why are they looking for us?"

How did one tell a five-year-old that people were trying to hurt her family and it was all her father's fault?

SEVEN

She didn't like the bleak expression that had entered Tyler's eyes. The sudden urge to hug him caught her by surprise. It also concerned her. At some point, her anger had cooled, leaving her vulnerable to other emotions. She needed to keep her emotional distance. Still, seeing him hurting was uncomfortable for her. He was doing his best to protect them.

It had taken some coaxing, but Bethany had given in and they were once again headed east. Most of the conversation had ceased. Annie didn't even try to talk. Partly because they were listening for the men to return, partly because they were all too tired and hungry to talk and partly because the thoughts whirling around inside her head were too heavy and chaotic for her to try to voice them yet.

They pushed on. Tyler was carrying Bethany, who had grown too tired to continue walking. Her thin arms had looped up and were clinging around his neck. He dropped a kiss on her head. Annabelle looked away, her eyes stinging at the tender action. She swallowed past the lump in her throat.

"Annabelle, do you have any water in that bag?" Tyler asked, his voice a soft rasp in the stillness.

Nodding, she slipped her purse over her neck so that it hung diagonally across her body. She opened it up and rifled inside the bag until her hand bumped into the bottled water she had placed in it earlier. It was slightly damp from condensation and cool to the touch. She pulled it out, quickly unscrewed the top and held it out to him. He carefully hoisted Bethany closer and removed one hand so he could drink. Then he offered the bottle to Bethany before handing it back to Annabelle. When their hands touched, she felt a subtle zing of electricity. She sucked in a breath. Her face warmed. Turning her head to hide her reaction, she took a drink then put the water back in her bag.

A little after six, they came into a small town. They took advantage of the rural setting to get something to eat at the gas station and freshen up. The man at the gas station looked at them suspiciously when they asked to make a phone call, but a couple of college students in the store heard them asking.

"You can use my phone, man." One of the young men handed Tyler his phone. Annabelle dug out Karl's card and handed it to him. She waited, nerves stretched taut, as he went to stand a bit apart from them to make the call. She could hear him talking but couldn't make out what he was saying.

A minute later he returned. "Thanks. I appreciate it." He handed the phone back to the college kid.

"No problem, dude."

They had done everything they had set out to do. Continually looking over their shoulders, they headed east again.

"Were you able to talk with Karl?"

He shook his head, his eyes continuing to roam their surroundings as they walked. Bethany walked between Tyler and Bethany, holding on to their hands. "No. I left a rather generic message telling him we were fine and heading east."

"I hope they are okay," she commented. He nodded but didn't say anything. He didn't need to. She saw his mouth tighten. He was as worried as she was.

"We need to find a place to stay for the night," Tyler said, his gaze still scouring the horizon.

Annabelle felt her shoulders slump. She was beyond exhausted. "I'm open to suggestions. I don't know that we want to use a credit card. And I don't think I have enough cash on me to spring for a hotel room."

"I might have enough. But I don't know if I'm comfortable with something as obvious as a hotel room, either."

They walked for a bit longer. Annabelle muttered prayers under her breath. *Just a place to sleep, Lord. Please. That's all we need.*

A few minutes later, she looked ahead and sucked in a breath. "How would that work?"

Tyler swung his head around to see what she was talking about. The grin that stretched across his face made her want to grin and laugh along with him. They were walking along the backyard of a house that had obviously been long abandoned, judging by the state of disrepair. That wasn't what she was looking at, though. She didn't think it would be safe to set foot inside the house.

The tree house, however, was another matter all together.

"Can we get up there safely?" Annie asked, her eyes glued to the little wooden house sitting majestically in a tree. It was perfect. It was also high in the air. She swallowed. Her gratefulness was dampened only by her fear of heights.

Tyler placed Bethany on the ground. His face considering, he walked around to the other side and ran his gaze up and down the tree in slow sweeps. "The ladder is still intact. We can take turns sleeping and keeping watch."

"Daddy, are we really going to get to sleep up there?" Bethany was wide-eyed with excitement, practically bouncing on her feet. Suddenly the weariness had been replaced by childish excitement. Annabelle smiled. Apparently a tree house topped her daughter's list of fun things to do. She eyed the tree house again. Sweat was starting to break out on her forehead. It wasn't her idea of fun. She couldn't see any other options, though.

Annabelle stepped next to Tyler and looked at the ladder. She wasn't as convinced as he was. True, the ladder was still there. Mostly. It was made up of slats of wood that had been nailed to the tree. There were two large gaps, but it should be passable.

"I'll go up last." Tyler narrowed his gaze

and tipped his head. His thinking pose. She remembered it well. "Annie, you go first. That way one of us will be at either end."

He didn't complete the thought. He didn't need to. She was thinking along the same lines. That way there would be a parent at either end to assist Bethany, whose short legs might have trouble reaching the places where a board was missing.

"Oh, Annie. Are you going to be all right with this?"

So he had remembered her slight aversion. Okay, that was an understatement. She wouldn't let that get in the way of finding a safe place to rest during the night. Instead of answering, she moved to the tree, inhaled deeply and said a prayer in her mind. Then she climbed the first rung.

Tyler's hand dropped onto her shoulder. A tingle vibrated where he touched. "We can keep looking."

She sighed. Then she set her jaw and climbed up the next rung. Then the next. The higher she climbed, the tighter her lungs felt. She ignored them. *One more step, Annabelle. Take another step.* By the time she arrived at the top, sweat was running down her back. She crawled off the ladder and onto the platform, gasping as she collapsed onto the wooden floor of the tree house. She took three calming breaths, then hauled herself to her hands and knees and crawled to the opening. Looking down, she slammed her eyes shut, fighting the swirling sensation behind her eyes.

You can do this. Focus on Bethany.

Peeling her lids apart, she looked down into Tyler's blue-gray eyes. Tenderness and concern stared back at her. Somehow, she found steadiness there. Which was ironic, considering their history.

"I'm okay. I'm good." She called down, "Bethy, come on up, sweetheart."

Annabelle held her breath as her tiny five-year-old wrinkled up her face in the most adorable expression of concentration and began her ascent. Tyler was right behind her, ready to catch her. The little girl struggled with the first gap. Tyler steadied her as she breached it. Why hadn't she ever noticed how strong he was?

Watching Tyler assist their daughter was surreal. She had thought the man didn't care, but caring was steeped in every move he made. The gentleness and love in his expression as he watched over Bethany tugged at her heart.

Which was the real Tyler?

Her thoughts were interrupted as Bethany reached the top. Annabelle lay on her stomach and stretched out her arms, assisting her daughter over the top. Tyler surged up after her.

Annabelle sat up, exhausted. Tyler plopped down next to her and hauled her into his arms for a brief hug. For a second, she allowed herself to relax against him, inhaling the familiar scent of mint and Tyler. It was comforting. She had the urge to snuggle deeper.

What was she doing? She stiffened and backed away, giving him a forced smile, ignoring the disappointment on his face. And the pulse pounding in her ears. "I'm okay. Really. Thanks."

For the first time she surveyed the inside of their lodgings and wrinkled her nose. A layer of dirt covered the floor. And a few leaves. Fortunately, the previous owners hadn't left anything. She wished she had her phone still so she could use the flashlight app to check for any other inhabitants. Like snakes. She shuddered at the thought.

Bethany was over the moon. She ran from one corner of the tree house to the other, peering out the windows, almost bouncing in her excitement. "This is so cool! Tasha and Nikki are going to be so jealous when I tell them."

If she tells them. Their situation pressed down on Annabelle again. Her daughter might never again see the twins. Or her grandmother and uncle. The knowledge latched on to her heart and tightened, like a fist. How did she explain that possibility when her little girl decided that she had had enough "adventure" and wanted to go home?

She pushed the worry from her mind. She just couldn't deal with it right now.

"We need to get some rest while we can," she whispered to Tyler.

He nodded. "You sleep first. I will stay awake and listen."

She took her purse off and used it as a pillow. Then, stretching out an arm, she bade Bethany to stretch out with her. Her daughter snuggled close, resting her head on Annabelle's outstretched arm. The sweetness of having her daughter safe and snuggled close overwhelmed Annabelle with gratitude.

"Thank You, Lord," she whispered, then closed her eyes to sleep.

Next to the wall, she heard a faint "Amen."

EIGHT

Bethany was making little sniffling sounds as she slept in her mother's arms. He'd expected more of an argument from her when Annabelle had called her over to lie down. The day's events had really tuckered out the poor kid. She didn't make a single protest.

He leaned back against the wall of their tiny shelter, his mind going back to watching Annabelle climb the ladder. He had been filled with worry that she would fall or faint or something. And pride. Because no matter what she was afraid of, Annie was a fighter. She always had been. He hadn't been at all surprised that she would put others ahead of herself. She had done that so many times in the past. Times he hadn't always appreciated. He could admit that now.

When he had hugged her earlier, he had only meant to tell her how proud he was of her, and how sorry he was that she had to do it at all. Those thoughts had melted away the moment she had relaxed against him. All at once, the memory of the years they had been in love overpowered him. Sadness that he had let life come between them seared into him. Not just life. His life. His choices. Choices that had robbed them of their love. Their marriage. And stolen his opportunity to watch his beautiful little girl grow up.

He'd missed so much. If they somehow survived this, he wanted the chance to be a part of her life again.

He'd destroyed his chances with her mother. He had known that, but the feeling had only been reinforced when she had pulled back out of his arms earlier. The cold that had made him shiver at the distance she put between them had nothing to do with the weather. The frustrating thing was he had been sure that she had felt something, too. But that was probably all in his mind.

Well, so what? The fact that his marriage was over in every way but legally came as no surprise. It was painful to admit it, but he did. He could still be a father, even if he couldn't be a husband.

Enough. He needed to stop being so maudlin. They were in a tough pickle right now, and he needed to use his time alone to think it through. Somehow, contract killers had found their way to the safe house where the marshals had been operating. Then, they had been ambushed.

The question was how? He knew that the place and vehicles hadn't been bugged. He remembered watching the marshals check everything for bugs. And he knew that the people employed to keep them safe had been thoroughly vetted. So the idea that one of them had been careless was ludicrous.

The marshals had also made it clear that everything was on a need-to-know basis. Karl hadn't even told the other marshals where exactly they were headed, just in case. Thinking about them brought back the memory of the recent events. He couldn't get the image of Rick slumped on the ground out of his mind. How was he? Had the police arrived in time to save him? And what about Karl and Stacy? Quietly, he said a quick prayer for their safety, feeling like a fraud. He had ignored God for so long, would He still hear Tyler's prayers?

He pondered their current circumstances for a few minutes. He was so deep in thought, in fact, that he almost missed the sound of approaching voices. One of those voices he recognized. Jim. The man who had chased them earlier was near.

Moving quietly, he reached over and placed a hand over Annie's mouth at the same time as he whispered, "Annie! Wake up!"

She jolted awake and jerked her elbow into his gut. He doubled over slightly. She was stronger than she looked. Bethany stirred, but didn't waken. Annie moved his hand off her mouth, and then kept holding on.

"Tyler?" she whispered fearfully. "What's—"

"Shh!"

She stilled. He could feel the tenseness of her body in the dark. She was listening. Her breathing was shallow and fast.

"Are you sure they came this way?" Tyler strained to hear the voices. The first man was obviously feeling out of sorts. "We've been walking and searching for hours. They have probably already been picked up by the police or the marshals by now."

So, the marshals were still alive. Or maybe he was talking about different marshals.

"Quit your complaining," a rough voice growled back. He knew that voice. Jim was standing right below them. "The man at the gas station said they had been through there. He recognized the kid's picture. They were headed this way. We know that they were going east. We'll just keep going and flashing the pictures around. Sooner or later, they are bound to mess up."

"I told you that going through the woman's house was a good idea. We got the pictures and we got the address for her mother."

Annie shifted beside him. He could feel the concern radiating off her. These men had been watching her mother. He put an arm around her, to comfort her. It felt natural to have her in his arms again. She didn't protest. Instead, she leaned into him. Her breathing grew harsh. Her shoulders trembled under his arm.

"It's a good thing the man watching the mother's house took note of the car that picked the woman up. But it would have been nicer still if we had an idea where they were heading."

The voices grew farther away as the men continued their search.

By the moonlight filtering in through the opening, Tyler could just barely make out the outline of Annie and Bethany. Annie's silhouette sat up, bringing her face into clearer focus. It was still mostly in shadows, but he could see the glint of her eyes. She looked mysterious. And angry.

"Those men, they were the ones who ransacked my house. And they were watching my mother? What kind of people are they, Tyler?"

He didn't hear any blame in her voice. She didn't ask him what he'd gotten them into. Although, he felt she would have had the right to ask that question. He was glad that some of her anger at him seemed to be dissipating. He also noticed that she hadn't moved away from him.

"This is why I have to testify," he murmured. "Men like that, men who would shoot someone in cold blood or threaten a child, they can't be allowed to go free. It doesn't matter how much we might fear them or what is happening."

She was so still in the darkness, he wondered what she was thinking. When she spoke again, he could hear the steel in her voice. "We have to do the right thing. Even if it costs us."

"Hopefully, this ordeal will be short, and we can return home." Although he had no idea what would happen then. For now, he had to live each moment as it came.

"What should we do?" she whispered now.

Good question. "Well, we know that those two guys are still heading east, searching for us. If we keep heading east, then we might run into those dudes again. That would be a huge mistake. Probably fatal for us."

Annie winced at his blunt words. "I don't know where Karl was taking us, but we've been heading east most of the journey. I'm worried if we don't go in that direction, how will we ever meet up with the marshals again? I'm sure that Stacy and Karl are still searching for us."

If they were alive.

Frustration bit at him. All he wanted to do was protect his family and put Wilson Barco behind bars for good so that he couldn't mess with people's lives anymore. Why was that so hard to do?

They spent the rest of the night taking turns watching. He didn't think either of them really got too much sleep, even if it was their turn. Near dawn, they both gave up the pretense and talked about their options.

"I think we have no choice but to head west. Or south. Definitely not east," Tyler said, leaning his head back against the wall again. Man, he was so tired, he wasn't sure if he was making any sense.

She bit her lip, bruising it. He fought the urge to lean over and kiss her. What was he thinking? Kissing? Really? With all that was happening, he needed to be clearheaded.

"I don't know, Ty." She pressed the heels of her palms against her temples. "It kind of feels like we are giving up if we head a different direction. Like we don't think we have a chance of being found again."

He hated to hear the defeat in her voice.

"If you have any other ideas, Annie, I would absolutely consider them." He wasn't being snarky. He was completely out of ideas. Annabelle had always been quick under pressure.

The horizon was starting to lighten up. They had made it through the night.

She blinked. Her lovely brown eyes widened. They sparkled with excitement. Just seeing that look come over her face was enough to send the adrenaline coursing through his veins. He knew what it meant.

Annie had a plan.

Annabelle could almost feel the excitement hopping off Tyler's skin as he waited to hear her plan. She'd forgotten how much she'd missed having someone listen to her like this. Tyler had never tried to talk her out of things. No, he had enjoyed the way her mind worked.

When had that stopped?

"What's your plan, Annie?"

She was right. No one knew her like Tyler did. Or had. She shifted slightly. She didn't have much of a plan, just an inkling of an idea.

"It's like this," she began, keeping her voice low so that she didn't wake up Bethany. It took some effort, because she was feeling so nervous and excited at the same time. "Those guys, they know we ran. They even have an idea of what we look like. And it's true we don't have a phone. But what if we were to go into a store and pick up one of those phones that you pay for by the month? We could get a phone, hold a conversation about heading to a specific place in front of the clerk. That way, if they happened to go in there, they would be led off track. We could call Karl and tell him where we are and get a place to meet. Even if we have to leave a message again, he'd have a way to contact us. And it wouldn't matter if we have to head in another direction, it will give them time to regroup and come for us."

She could see he was considering it. "That should work. And if we keep to the side roads, and watch out for any traffic, it might just be workable."

"Plus, we would have a way to call the police if we did get into trouble."

They waited in the tree house for an additional two hours, just until the sun was up and Bethany had awakened. They ate quickly, finishing off a bottle of water bought from the gas station. Annabelle was torn between relief that they hadn't seen anyone else and frustration at not knowing where danger could be lurking. She absolutely had no desire to encounter the men who wanted to kill her, her daughter and her husband. However, it was nerve-racking needing to keep up constant vigilance.

Climbing down the tree house was easier than getting the nerve to go up the thing had been. The fact that she had a case of cabin fever might have had something to do with it. All she wanted to do was move.

They started hiking, keeping themselves off the most well-traveled roads. The sense of adventure had long since faded. Even Bethany was quiet this morning. Every now and then the little girl would heave a sigh of giant proportions. As serious as the situation was, Annabelle couldn't help but smile at her daughter. She was so cute when she was feeling the need to be dramatic.

After several hours, they came to a small town. They entered a drugstore and picked up some food and some more water. And a small pay-by-the-minute cell phone. As they stood in line, Tyler and Annabelle held a conversation, as planned.

"I think we should head toward Fort Wayne," he said.

She nodded, wincing slightly at his overly loud voice. Really, he was a horrible actor. "We could do that. That seems to make sense."

By the time they reached the bored clerk, Annabelle was clenching her teeth. They were so out in the open here. Yes, it had been her plan, but she wanted nothing more than to bolt out of the store and hide with Bethany and Tyler. Any moment now, one of the men after them could waltz right through those sliding doors. What would they do then? She doubted if the men would hesitate to shoot. Or kidnap Bethany. A shudder worked its way done her spine.

Tyler casually reached over and grabbed her hand. She startled. Forcing herself to calm down, she squeezed his hand to let him know she was all right. He raised an eyebrow at her, concern radiating from his blue-gray gaze. She smiled at him. He watched her for a minute before nodding and releasing her hand. Immediately, she wanted to reach out and grab his hand again. Which was ridiculous.

She curled her fingers into her palm and focused her attention on her little girl.

Finally, they were on their way.

"Let's get a few miles between us and this store before we try to set up the phone and call." Tyler hefted up Bethany into his arm and grabbed Annabelle's hand again. She allowed him to lead them back into the shadows.

They walked for another twenty minutes in silence. Annabelle's thoughts whirled chaotically in her mind. Tyler's voice broke through.

"You are not going to like this." Tyler's statement came out of nowhere.

"What? I've not liked a number of things recently. Can you be a bit more specific?" She allowed the sarcasm to drip in her tone, knowing that Tyler would find it amusing. Sure enough, he chuckled softly.

His chuckle dwindled, though, as he nodded his head to the right. "You're not going to like that."

Annabelle followed where he was indicating. The pit of her stomach dropped out.

There. Was. No. Way.

But she knew that he was right. The bridge that stretched out across the fast-moving stream was the best way to continue heading east and putting distance between them and the people who wanted to cash in on their deaths.

It was also the flimsiest excuse for a bridge that she had ever seen.

NINE

Her heart rate went into overdrive as they approached the bridge. The stream was only about thirty feet across. And it didn't look that deep. Beneath the surface of the rippling, clear water, the rocks settled on the bottom were visible. What really bothered her was the speed at which it roared past. She was a good swimmer, but she knew that she would be swept away in that current. And what about Bethany?

The little girl had just started to learn to swim this summer. Before that, she'd been afraid to get into the water.

"I am sorry, Annie. I think it's our best option. We can move on, though, and try something else." Tyler. Trying to be understanding.

Her guilt shot up a notch. She was not going to be the one holding them back.

"No. You're right. This is our best option.

I need to get over myself and do it." She clenched her jaw tight. She could do this.

"That's not what I meant. You know that." Now he sounded offended.

She cringed. She knew that wasn't what he had been getting at. Facing her fears made her snap. "No, really. I need to do this."

Without another word, they approached the bridge. A stiff breeze would rattle it. A cold sweat broke out all over her. She had no idea how she would manage this.

"Look, it won't be that bad," Tyler insisted. "There are handrails. And most of the wood is intact. Step over the parts that look rotted."

That looked like most of the bridge.

She looked at him. He must have seen her fear. He stepped up to her and rubbed his hands up and down her arms. "You can do this, Annie. I will do whatever I can to help you out. Let me get Bethany across and then I will help you."

Without thinking, she leaned forward so that her forehead rested on his chest. His hands gently squeezed her arms. Sucking in a fortifying breath, she stepped back.

"I can handle a bridge, Tyler. Fear or no fear. I will be right behind you." The words sounded good. She hoped that she could go through with them.

He glanced deep into her eyes, but finally he nodded. He turned and held out a hand to Bethany. "Okay, Bethany, let's see if we can cross this bridge together, honey. I want you to hold my hand, do you understand?"

Bethany had apparently caught some of the vibes. Her eyes were round with fear as she nodded. "I don't wanna."

Her favorite phrase lately.

"I know you don't, bug. I wish you didn't have to. But I need you to do this. We need to keep going so the bad men don't find us." Her eyes grew even bigger. Annabelle waited for the tears to come. To her surprise, the tiny girl reached for her daddy's hand and let him lead her across the bridge.

The bridge was every bit as rickety as she had feared. She trembled as she watched her husband and child slowly cross over the vicious water flowing below. Her heartbeat was heavy in her chest as she kept up a constant litany of prayer. She stepped onto the bridge when they reached the middle. A blast of wind hit them suddenly. Was the bridge shaking? Or was it just her? The bridge quivered below her feet. She placed her hands on the rails and took a step. The rails and the wood beneath her feet vibrated with each and every step she took.

Don't look down. Don't look down.

She looked down. The sight of the water rushing below nearly brought her down to her knees. Her stomach heaved. She jerked her head up, striving to keep her eyes on the bridge and her husband's back. He was right in front of her. He and Bethany had almost reached the other side.

Even as she watched, he took another careful step. His foot went through the rotting wood. Bethany screamed. Annabelle's heart stopped.

"Shh. It's okay, Bethany. Just a bad piece of wood. Let's keep going."

Where did he get it from? The man had nerves of steel. He'd been shot at, several times, seen his boss murdered, been brought into hiding and now was walking across this death trap of a bridge, and still his voice was calm and reassuring. As if this was a normal afternoon walk for him. A feeling of admiration spread through her.

She was frozen. They made it to the other side. She stood where she was, feeling the bridge sway and hearing each individual creek.

She drew in a deep breath and edged forward. One step. Another. Partway across, she saw the place where Tyler had lost his footing. Holding her breath, she stepped around it. She was almost to the other side, when she heard Tyler shout.

"Behind you! Get down!"

A shot rang out. It bounced off the tree next to his head.

She looked behind her. Jim and his friend had figured out that they were being tricked. She dropped to her hands and knees, feeling the bridge give a slight bounce as her weight hit it.

She couldn't believe she had just done that.

Another shot. This time, when she looked ahead, she saw that Tyler had shoved Bethany behind the tree. He was kneeling at the other end of the bridge, hand outstretched. Desperation stood out starkly in his eyes.

With a burst of speed she hadn't known she was capable of, she scrambled across the bridge on her hands and knees. If she was going to die, it wasn't going to be because she had waited for death to come and get her.

As soon as she was close to him, Tyler reached out and grabbed her, pulling her the rest of the way over. Together, they ran to where Bethany was.

Another shout behind her made Annabelle swing around. Her mouth dropped open. There was a gap in the bridge. Jim was lying flat on the bridge, his Illinois baseball cap nearly falling off his head. The other man was nowhere to be seen. Right in front of Jim, though, there was a gaping hole. She knew immediately what had happened. Jim and friend had obviously decided to follow after them across the bridge. They had also apparently lacked the sense to move slowly.

"We can't stay here."

Urgency colored Tyler's voice. Bethany was in tears.

Tyler picked up Bethany in his uninjured arm. "We have to get away from here. Far away."

Tyler couldn't believe how close they had come to getting caught. The look on Annie's face when she had frozen on the bridge had terrified him. Then he had spied the men running up behind them. He didn't think he'd ever forget that image—a man holding a gun, aimed right at them, while Annie's back was turned to him.

She could have been hit. Maybe injured. Or worse.

He couldn't let himself be drawn into thinking about that right now. He had more important things to do. Such as locating the marshals.

"Let's get that cell phone set up and try the marshals."

She searched him with her eyes. "I am going to have nightmares about that bridge for the rest of my life."

He glanced down at her. "Me, too. I think my heart stopped when you fell to your knees. The way it bounced! Not to mention watching those men run onto the bridge, shooting." He shook his head fiercely as if trying to shake off the memory.

Bethany hiccupped into his shoulder. Annie tightened her lips and grabbed the phone out of her bag. "I am not even sure if the thing is already charged. We may have wasted our time."

He thought about it. "Yeah, but it's worth a shot."

Shrugging, Annie unboxed the phone and turned it on. It took ten minutes, but she was able to get it set up and add the airtime.

"It doesn't have a lot of battery." She showed him the phone. The battery icon was almost empty.

"It's better than nothing." He hoped it was enough.

Pulling out Karl's number, she quickly punched in the digits and hit Send. She put it on speaker, so Tyler could hear it, too. It was answered almost immediately.

"Hello?"

"Karl? It's Annabelle." Tyler could see the tears welling in her eyes.

Hearing the voice of the marshal relaxed something inside of him. At least they knew he had survived. He had not allowed his mind to go there, but the thought had been constantly in the background the past day and half.

"Annabelle? Where are you? Are Tyler and Bethany with you?"

"Hey, Karl. Tyler here. Yes, we're all fine. Although we have had a few close calls. We saw Rick was hurt. How is he? And Stacy?"

"Rick will be out of commission for a few weeks, but he'll be fine. Stacy is here with me. We've both been concerned about you."

Annie and Tyler gave as clear directions as they could. The bridge they crossed was actually a landmark that Karl recognized. "I know that bridge. Crossed it a few times myself when I was hiking in the area as a teen. I used to live around here. I'm only about an hour from you. Keep heading east. If you hit Garman Road, follow it. We'll track you dow—"

Karl's voice was cut off. Annie looked at

the phone in her hand. It was no surprise when she informed Tyler that they had no battery left.

"I guess we keep walking." Tyler wanted nothing more than to slow down, but that wasn't a choice.

Twenty minutes later, they hit Garman Road. Both Tyler and Annie let out sighs as they spotted the name. It was a two-lane highway with a constant stream of traffic. They continued walking until a dark Ford Taurus pulled out of the line of traffic onto the narrow shoulder beside them. He had never seen the car before. Tyler was ready to grab his family and bolt when the window rolled down and he saw Stacy looking at them. Karl was in the driver's seat.

"Care for a ride?" Stacy's words were casual, but the skin around her eyes was tight. They were the eyes of someone who had been worried.

Tyler nodded and opened the back door. A booster chair was sitting in the middle for Bethany. He let his daughter in, then gestured for Annie to follow her. Once they were both inside, he jogged around to the other side of the vehicle. Karl turned on the blinker. It might be a minute or so before there was a break that would allow Karl to merge back onto the highway.

Nothing had ever felt as good as sinking into car seats in the back of an air-conditioned car. He barely had the energy to strap himself in before he slumped down in the seat and closed his eyes, letting out a sigh.

"I was expecting a different car," Annie said softly.

He opened his eyes a crack. That's right. They had left Iowa with three distinctly different vehicles.

Stacy turned partially around in her seat. "Our other vehicles have obviously been made. We still don't know how they found us."

Tyler straightened in his seat. "We do."

Briefly, he told the marshals about the past day, including the conversation that he and Annie had overheard while they were hiding in the tree house. "I wondered about that. But no one was spotted following us. The good thing is, they have no idea where you are headed, and this is a totally different vehicle."

"I'm just relieved that Rick wasn't killed," Tyler said. "I think I would have felt guilty for the rest of my life if he had died."

To his surprise, Annabelle reached around

Bethany and touched his shoulder. "You had no control over this situation, Tyler. I know it's awful, but you are as much a victim of it as we are. I can't even think about what you went through, seeing your boss killed that way."

He grabbed on to her words like a lifesaver. Could she really mean it? "But my job—"

"Does not give anyone the right to harm you or anyone connected to you."

"She's right, Tyler." Stacy shifted so she could turn in her seat and see them. "None of this is your fault."

A glance flickered between Karl and Stacy. He could see Karl's arm move. And Stacy blush. Was he holding her hand? Tyler peered around Bethany at Annabelle. He grinned. Her eyes were narrowed as she gazed speculatively at the two in the front seat. So she saw it, too.

The silence that fell was heavy, thick with the emotions of the adults in the car.

Karl broke the silence. "It's time we told you about where you will be going. There's a little Amish community in Ohio. It's in a small farming town called Harvest. There's a large number of Amish and Mennonite families settled there. You will be going in the program as Ty and Annie Miller. You need to start thinking of yourselves that way. There is no more Tyler and Annabelle."

Things were starting to feel real very quickly. Karl continued to speak.

"You are going to be a young married couple who have decided to join the Amish church but have not yet been baptized. That should help you out of situations where you come across a cultural tradition or taboo. Plain folk will be forgiving since you are still learning. You will be staying with Abraham and Julia Beiler. They will supposedly be old friends of yours who have invited you to stay with them while you make the transition to Amish life."

"How much do they know?" They had to know something, obviously. US Marshals were asking them to house people in their home. Complete strangers.

Stacy replied. "They know that you are in the witness protection program. And they know that you are not really Amish. We didn't tell them the entire story. But they wouldn't be surprised. They, too, are in the witness protection program."

Tyler felt his jaw come unhinged. They were being placed with other program members? That seemed a bit unusual.

"What else?" Annie asked.

"Well, let's see… Julia has two children. Her son, William, is fourteen. He's a nice young man, responsible and very helpful. Her daughter, Kayla, is seven. I think she'll be a good friend for Bethany."

Bethany's ears picked up this last comment. She lifted her head from the toys that she had found on her seat. "Does Kayla like to swim? I am learning to swim this summer."

Stacy grinned. Tyler understood. His daughter was too cute to resist. "I have no clue if she swims, honey. You'll have to ask."

Nodding, Bethany lost interest in the conversation and returned to her toys.

"Where was I?" Stacy tapped her chin. "Well, Abraham was a police officer for about a decade or so. Although he was raised Amish, right, Karl?"

The blond man at the wheel nodded. "Yup. He was recently wounded. Oh, and the bishop knows that you are in the program. He is a rather forward-thinking man. He agreed to allow you to have sanctuary in his district. I promised him you'd try to conform as best as you could."

Tyler expected as much. Annie had a hesitant look on her face. "Everything will work out, Annie. We can do this."

She rolled her eyes. "You have no idea, Tyler. But I promised to try. So I will."

"We'll be there in a few hours. It's a nine-hour drive from where we were staying in Iowa. We're in Indiana right now."

"I should be able to pull onto the road after the red truck passes." Karl craned his head to watch the progress of the truck, his hands starting to turn the wheel.

Before he could pull back onto the road, a bullet hit the side of the car. Bethany screamed. Annie put her arms around her daughter in an attempt to shelter her. Tyler was dimly aware of Stacy calling in the attack on her radio.

The shooter was somewhere off to the right, staying out of sight.

Suddenly, Tyler realized that their heads were above the back seat. Within sight of anyone with a gun. Without pausing, he reached over and unbuckled Bethany.

"What are you doing?" Annie screamed at him.

"Guns! Annie, they have guns."

Horror replaced the surprise on her face. Without another word, she snatched open the latch on her own seat belt. Then she pulled her screaming daughter onto the floor with her. Tyler ducked down.

The back window shattered.

Bethany started sobbing. "I scared, Daddy! I scared!"

He reached over and ran his hand down the top of her head. "I know, baby. I need you to be brave. Hang on tight to Mommy."

That wasn't going to be a problem—he could see that she had a death grip on her mother. And Annie obviously was holding on to her as hard as she could. He knelt beside them on the floor, covering them as much as possible with his own body.

Please, God, protect them. Keep them safe.

The spontaneous prayer was a cry from deep within his soul. He would do whatever he could to spare them as much pain as humanly possible. If that meant taking a bullet for them, then that's exactly what he would do.

The tires squealed as Karl yanked sharply on the wheel, pulling the car out onto the road. A bullet smashed through the rear passenger window, sprinkling glass over the back seat and the three people crouched on the floor. Stacy screamed.

"Stacy!" Karl yelled, the car jerking.

Stacy sat up. "I'm okay. It missed me."

"Stay down," Karl yelled. Tyler could hear the fear in his voice. It had to be hard for him, seeing the woman he had feelings for in danger. Tyler knew exactly how he felt. He pulled Annabelle and Bethany closer. Karl's jaw was clenched as he kept driving. A minute later, they heard sirens. Sitting up, Tyler looked back and saw two police cars driving along the shoulder. Tyler and Annie relaxed their positions. The top of their heads touched, right above the daughter they were trying to protect. For a moment, neither moved. Tyler needed this connection with her right now. Knowing how close they had come to being injured, he needed to know that Annie and Bethany were unharmed.

Five minutes later, Karl had pulled off the road. The marshals quickly took stock of their situation. Stacy had a spot of blood on her left shoulder where a piece of glass had nicked her, but she was fine. Karl looked at the wound, his face pale and tense, while she talked to him in a calming voice. Several times, her right hand moved to touch his cheek. Karl hugged her briefly. When he released her, he turned to them, his calm marshal face firmly back in place.

Tyler could still see the shadows in the man's eyes. Shadows brought by seeing a loved one in danger. He peeked at Annabelle and Bethany out of the corner of his eye. They were fine, sitting huddled together. He knew how Karl felt, all too well.

Karl might look unmoved by the events of the past hour, but Annabelle had seen his reaction when he'd thought Stacy had been hurt. No matter how calm he was now, it was obvious that the tall blond marshal was in love with the brunette Stacy. Watching their interactions as he took care of her shoulder, Annabelle was certain that the woman returned his feelings.

How would she feel if anything happened to Tyler?

It was not a comfortable question. Not too long ago, Annabelle was sure that she wanted no part of Tyler back in her life. She had the reasons memorized. He was unreliable. He put his work above his family. He didn't care enough.

The Tyler she was seeing now, however, was not that way. He had put himself in harm's way for them several times. His care and concern for them was real. She knew it was. The way he had protected her and Bethany several times already proved that. He had changed in the time they had been separated.

What would she do if anything happened to him?

She recalled the way she had felt when she saw the blood on his arm earlier. Granted, it was not a serious wound. But if it had been? If she lost him, how would she react?

She had to be honest with herself. If something did happen to Tyler, no matter how angry she was, she would be devastated. Not just because he was Bethany's father, either. She had to take care. It would be far too easy to find herself falling for him all over again.

And that thought terrified her.

TEN

Tyler had thought that they would never make it to the Amish community. At least, not alive. Karl had been mostly silent for the past few hours, only talking to answer questions or to give necessary information. Stacy had tried to talk with him, but his answers were mostly single-word replies. Tyler didn't envy the man. He clearly had feelings for Stacy. He obviously hated that Stacy was in danger, but he also respected her as a marshal. Tyler recalled his own reaction when Annabelle had been hurt. His response had been to emotionally and physically withdraw from his family. A decision that he was now regretting. Knowing what Karl might be going through, Tyler had allowed the man his privacy. Several times, he'd exchanged concerned glances with Annie. She'd obviously noticed Karl's withdrawal. And though she hadn't said anything about it, he had no doubt that Annie was aware of the full reason behind it. She was a very observant woman, his Annie was.

Except that she was most definitely not his Annie. Not anymore. A fact that was getting harder to remember the more time they spent in one another's company. She fascinated him in so many ways. He had to keep reminding himself of why he had needed to let her go in the first place.

He could change jobs if they ever got out of the witness protection program.

The thought stunned him momentarily. And it was tempting. Very tempting. He did not let himself dwell on the thought, however, knowing that he had an obligation to fulfill. His current job was his best way of going about that. No matter how much he was growing to hate it.

Karl pulled up a long driveway. It was gravel, and Tyler could hear the rocks crunching beneath the wheels of the car. Dust billowed around them. It had been a few days since it had rained. A large white two-story farmhouse loomed before them. Alongside the driveway, wood was stacked. The family was already preparing for the harsh months of winter. A clothesline on a pulley system ran from the edge of the porch to the top of the garage. Sheets, dresses, shirts and trousers snapped and waved in the breeze.

Near the top of the drive, Karl parked the vehicle. Beyond it, Tyler saw an enclosed buggy in the barn.

When he'd envisioned Amish communities, he'd somehow pictured houses closer together. These houses were on large plots of land. Not only that, but it was also obvious that while most of the houses on the street were owned by Amish, not all of them were.

"Are all the Amish homes white?" he asked in a low voice.

"Around here they are," Karl responded. "I am not one hundred percent sure, but that may be one of the things decided by their bishop. Things like color of clothing and such can be decided by him. So, you might have two districts side by side with different rules."

"Hmm." Interesting information to tuck away in the back of his mind.

Karl and Stacy opened their doors and Tyler followed suit. Then he jogged around the car and opened Annie's door for her. She unfastened Bethany and helped the child out of the car. The solemn group approached the house.

As they walked up onto the porch, the

door was opened by an attractive woman of around thirty. Her lovely golden-brown hair was tucked beneath a white bonnet-type hat. He couldn't remember the name of it. The strings were untied and hung over her shoulders. The little bonnet reminded him of a teacup, with the flat back and the round shape of the sides. The woman was dressed in a calf-length blue dress with a white apron on it.

"I am happy that you have arrived. Please come in. I am Julia. My husband will be here shortly."

The tired family moved inside the house. The late afternoon was warm, but the house was surprisingly cool.

It was a beautiful house. All wooden floors and handcrafted furniture. There were, of course, no lamps or electric appliances. The light streaming into the kitchen was all natural. The walls were bare, except for a few oil lamps. No pictures were hung on them. Nor were there any curtains on the windows. But still the place felt like a home. The floor plan was open, and the living room was larger than he was used to seeing in a house. There was a large china cabinet with a full set of china situated near the side wall in the combined kitchen-and-dining area. And he could see quilts on several of the chairs.

"You have a lot of open space here," he commented.

"We need the space," Julia said. "It's for when we have church."

Tyler raised his eyebrows. He looked around at the others in the room. Apparently, Karl and Stacy both understood what she was saying because they nodded. He felt foolish for asking, but if he was going to pretend to be Amish for a while, he should probably know about this, as well. He glanced at Annie and saw the same blank look on her face that was probably on his. So he wasn't the only one. When she turned her head, their eyes met. And held. Electricity shimmered in the air between them. She broke the connection first, cheeks reddening.

He rubbed the back of his neck, feeling uncomfortable. His neck was warm. His cheeks and ears were probably red, too. He pulled his mind back to what they had been discussing. There were so many things about the Amish culture he didn't know. It was like he was in school and didn't know the material the day before the test. He felt ridiculous needing to ask about the most basic things. But he didn't let that stop him. This was too important to let pride stand in the way. He could literally risk his family's life if he didn't have some sort of understanding of the Amish culture.

"I hate to sound ignorant," he said. "This is all very new to me. You have church in your house?"

Julia didn't seem to mind all the questions. In fact, she grinned at him.

"I know it seems a little bit strange." She chuckled a little. "When I first came to an Amish community, I was a little startled by it, as well. Now, it seems natural. Just as it should be. Amish homes are built with a wide-open floor plan so that every family in the district can host the church service at least once a year. There are almost twenty families in our district. We have church every other week. On the weeks that we don't have church, that's a visiting day when we can go and visit relatives and friends."

"Where do all the people sit?" Bethany asked, joining the conversation. Her face scrunched up as she thought of something that she didn't care for. "Does everybody have to stand during the whole church service?"

Julia laughed again. Annie covered her mouth so she wouldn't laugh at her daughter. Tyler ruffled the soft blond hair on top of her head. He got such a kick out of listening to the way her mind worked.

A pout started to form. She must have thought the adults were laughing at her.

"Don't feel bad, bug. I want to know that, too," he told her with a wink.

Julia was shaking her head. "No, we don't stand for the whole service. There is a set of wooden benches that are brought around and set up in the house on Saturday evening. We have what is called our church wagon and that is the trailer that carries the benches. Church Sundays are always a fun time."

Bethany didn't look like she was convinced.

The child continued to pepper Julia with questions. It soon became clear that Julia had a lot of practice handling an inquisitive five-year-old. She answered the questions with patience and good humor.

The back door flew open and another little girl dashed into the room. She was three inches or so taller than Bethany. The girl crashed to a stop when she saw that they had company. Her eyes popped with excitement.

"Mommy! Who are they?"

Julia turned to Tyler's family. "I would like you to meet my daughter, Kayla. Kayla is seven years old and in second grade. My son, William, will be home soon. He is fourteen. He and my husband are out working on chores in the barn."

Kayla had apparently lost interest in the conversation. All of her attention was focused squarely on Bethany. She walked over to stand beside the younger girl, giving her a quick inspection.

"I'm Kayla," she said, forgetting that her mother had already introduced her. "What's your name?"

Bethany ducked her head, shy for once. "I'm Bethany. I'm gonna be six."

Tyler and Annie exchanged laughing glances. "Bethany," Annie said, "you just turned five a few months ago."

Bethany heaved a dramatic sigh and rolled her eyes. "I know that, Mommy. But that means that I'm going to be six next."

A few minutes later, Abraham Beiler arrived with William. Tyler liked them right off. Abraham was not the most talkative fellow one could meet, but Tyler could tell that he was an intelligent man. He tried to imagine the man in the dark Amish trousers and the full beard as a cop. It was there in the eyes, he decided. Those eyes said that he had seen far more pain and despair than he had ever wanted to in his lifetime. Tyler would never ask. He respected the man's privacy. Not to mention the fact that he had seen his own share of grief.

Before he left, Karl pulled Annie and Tyler, or Ty, aside. "I'm giving you guys a phone to use in case of an emergency. It is for emergency use only. This placement will only work if you two do your best to fit in. That means phones are out. Do not try to contact anyone from your old life."

He glanced over at Annie when he said that. Ty grimaced. Probably because she had someone worth contacting. Everyone he had was here in the program with him. That was a little sad to think about, but it worked out well, considering the circumstances.

"Will we see you again?" Annie asked.

"Oh, yeah. I will check in on you. And if you ever feel that you are in danger, I will come, or Jonathan or another marshal. You are not in this alone."

Karl's phone buzzed. He pulled his phone out of his pocket and read the text. Tyler was startled to see a huge grin break across the man's face. And relieved. The man had been so somber for the past few hours, the expression was a welcome change.

"I have some good news," Karl announced to the group at large. "Jonathan texted me to say that he and his wife, Celeste, have a beautiful baby girl, and Celeste is doing wonderful."

The mood of the group lightened after that information. Putting his phone away, Karl appeared more relaxed than he had been. He talked to Tyler for a few minutes more. Tyler let his gaze drift over to Annie for a few seconds. Stacy was with her. Whatever they were talking about, it looked intense. Realizing that Karl was still speaking, he yanked his attention back to him.

Karl and Stacy left. Julia showed them to their rooms. Tyler's room was on the first floor, but Annie and Bethany were both on the second floor. Abraham handed Tyler some clothes similar to what he and William were wearing. Annie and Bethany followed Kayla and Julia upstairs to try on some Amish clothes.

Abraham invited Ty to go out to the barn with him and William to start getting him acclimated to his new life. Karl had said that they weren't alone. And it was true.

But at the moment, surrounded by people and a way of life he wasn't familiar with, it sure felt like he was.

Annabelle woke up the next morning feeling disoriented. It took her a few moments to realize where she was. She reached over on the bedside table for her phone out of habit. *Oh, right*, she remembered as her hand touched an empty surface. No technology.

This was going to be interesting.

Not that she was glued to her phone or anything. She was just used to being able to look up the time and the weather anytime she wanted to. Or search the internet for obscure facts if she had time to kill. Or catch up on whatever was trending on Facebook.

Okay, maybe she was a little too attached to technology.

She lay still for a few minutes, thinking back on her conversation with Stacy. It had been strange. She'd asked the female marshal how she was feeling. The other woman had given her a smile.

"I'm fine, really. Don't worry about me."

"Karl seemed to be concerned," Annabelle had blurted without thinking.

Stacy had grinned, her cheeks growing pink. "I should have known we wouldn't be able to hide it. Karl and I have been seeing each other for a while now."

"Isn't it hard, dating someone when you have such dangerous occupations?"

When Stacy had laughed softly, Annabelle had realized just how rude her questions might sound. "I'm sorry. I shouldn't—"

"No, I understand. Look, yes, our jobs are dangerous. One of us might get hurt someday. Or worse. I believe that when you are blessed enough to have someone you love in your life, you shouldn't waste it. Love is too precious."

She had given Annabelle a significant look. What was her message? Annabelle felt uncomfortable with the memory now, sure she didn't really want to know.

She dragged herself out of bed and looked at the dresses that Julia had found for her. There were several in various pastel shades. She picked up the first one. It was a plain lavender-colored dress. Although she normally went for brighter colors, it was a lovely hue. She put it on and then tied the white apron over it. It felt strange wearing a dress after so many years. And a dress with elbow-length sleeves, too. She usually wore sleeveless tops in the summer. Or T-shirts. Warily, she glanced down at her feet. The dress came to three inches above her ankles. Her scars didn't show. Mostly. But if she stretched up, the dress might ride up enough to show them.

Black stockings it was. Grimacing, she pulled the stockings on her feet. Immediately, she felt less self-conscious. There was no way the scars would show now. Not dressed like this.

The hair. What had Julia said about her hair? She would have to put it up. Apparently, Amish women never cut their hair. Julia had told her she could braid it and put it up or wear it in a bun. Annabelle chose to wear it in a braid. She knew how to make a neat braid. Her buns were always messy and tended to come undone.

After a frustrating ten minutes, she had her hair up and the starched white *kapp* that Julia had given her perched on top. She wished there was a mirror to see herself. She felt like she was playing dress-up. With a sigh, she realized that she had no reason to delay any longer. She went to Bethany's room to help her daughter get dressed for the day.

It soon became apparent that Bethany thought dressing Amish was great fun. She was going to look just like Kayla. Bethany was bouncing with glee as Annie fixed her hair like Kayla had worn hers the night before. When she saw the little *kapp*, Bethany squealed and clapped her hands.

"Really? I get my own little hat? I'm gonna look just like Kayla!"

Laughing, Annie put it on her head. "Yes,

you get your own little hat. You look like Kayla and like Bethany."

"Hurry, Mommy! I want to go see her!"

There was nothing more that needed to be done.

Holding out her hand to her daughter, she said, "Let's go and join the others, shall we?"

"Whee!" Bethany caught her mother's hand and skipped to the door, pulling Annie along with her. Annie allowed her daughter to drag her down the stairs and into the kitchen. The poor thing had been through a rough few days. She couldn't find the heart to try and temper her excitement.

"Bethany!"

"Kayla!"

The two girls embraced each other like they were best friends who hadn't seen each other for months. All the adults smiled.

"Let me look at my Amish girls." Tyler strode forward, grinning. Annie couldn't help it. An answering grin tugged up the corners of her mouth. She turned away so he wouldn't see it. Or see how affected she was by the sight of him. Why was her heart pounding?

"Look at me, Daddy!" Bethany twirled for her father.

Tyler picked her up and cuddled her close, placing a kiss on her bonneted head. Annabelle's heart melted. Whatever issues they had in the past, she could no longer deny that Tyler truly loved his daughter. What had happened to change him all those years ago?

"You sure do look plain," Julia commented.

She couldn't get over the change in Tyler. It suddenly struck her that he was growing a beard. Of course, he had not been able to shave in the past few days. She hadn't even really noticed the extra growth. But now, as he stood before her in dark trousers and a blue shirt with dark suspenders on, she could see it. He had shaved the mustache that had also started to come in. And sometime between last night and this morning, his hair, which he had always worn on the longish side, had been cut. Not the usual cut, either. He now had the same haircut that Abraham sported. Part of her wanted to giggle. The other realized that it didn't matter how Tyler dressed or groomed himself, he was still a very handsome man. One that had the ability to make her pulse skip. Even after everything they'd been through.

That was not the way she wanted to be thinking.

The group sat down to eat a light breakfast. After breakfast, the men left to go to the barn.

Tyler paused on his way out. He put a hand on her elbow and led her over to the window.

"How are you doing? I have been worried about you."

She blinked. "Worried about me? Why? I'm doing fine. It was nice to get a full night's sleep in a real house."

He smiled, but she could see the worry was still there. "Annie, I'm serious. I know that this is a safe place for us. Even so, I keep thinking of all the close calls we've had. Those people coming for me have been relentless. And I am feeling horrible dragging you and Bethany into this whole mess."

"Hush." She placed her fingers over his lips. The skin where they touched tingled. She snatched her hand away, face heating up. For a second, she forgot what she had been planning on saying. "I know that we could still be in danger. And I know that I was really angry with you just a couple of days ago. But, Tyler, this mess is not your fault. You didn't know that your boss was working with criminals. Nor did you have any idea what you were walking into. That's life."

Her heart thudded in her chest as the look on his face warmed. "You are amazing, you know that?"

Embarrassed, she decided that they were

getting just a little too serious. She placed a hand on her hip and gave her head a saucy toss, which probably looked silly with a *kapp* on. "Yes, I am amazing, mister. Glad you finally caught on."

Tyler grinned at her antics. She relaxed a little, happy that she had chased some of the seriousness from his face. Then, before she knew what he was about, he bent and placed a warm kiss on her cheek.

"Oh, I always knew that you were amazing. I was just making sure you knew it, too."

With a last wink, he sauntered away and grabbed the straw hat that was hanging on a hook by the back door. Then he was gone, off to find Abraham in the barn. Annie stared after him, her mouth hanging open in surprise. Without thinking, she reached up and placed her hand over the spot he'd kissed. It still felt warm.

Julia bustled by, tossing Annie a smirk as she passed.

Annie blew out a breath, hard. She placed a hand on her heart, feeling the heavy beat.

So much for not letting herself be affected by his charm. Oh, she was in so much trouble.

ELEVEN

"I don't wanna." Bethany folded her arms across her chest and pouted.

Here we go again, Annabelle thought, frustration beginning to stir inside her. They had been living in the Beilers' home for a week now. Bethany had been enchanted with the old farmhouse for the first few days. Her first buggy ride had thrilled the little girl. Bethany felt like a grown-up as she helped her mother and Julia with the chores around the house. Annie sighed. She'd never enjoyed helping with laundry and baking so much. She understood it. Bethany must have felt like she was on an extended camping trip. Plus, Kayla, Julia's daughter, was helping. And Bethany adored Kayla. She also loved the cows and the horses.

And the chickens. Annie was tempted to roll her eyes at the thought. Her daughter had discovered that the chickens didn't mind being carried around. She had adopted one of them as her own. She'd named the hen Mrs. Feathers.

Julia and Abraham were very gentle and understanding when Bethany would run after the large white bantam and carry her around like she was an overgrown cat. Of course, the line had to be drawn when Bethany wanted to bring the chicken into the house with her.

"*Nee*, we do not have chickens in the house," Julia had told her gently when the child first brought her inside.

Annie was sure she'd see a temper tantrum. Instead, fourteen-year-old William had coaxed Bethany and her new pet outside with him. Annie and Julia had laughed about it after they had left the house.

This morning, however, Bethany had announced that she was ready to go home. No amount of pleading or arguing with logic would work. Nor would bribing her daughter. She'd tried everything she could to gain her child's cooperation, but Bethany wasn't having it.

"Come on, Bethany. You've worn a *kapp* every day we've been here. You know that Kayla and Julia wear one, too. And I have been wearing one, too. You said you liked it. Remember?"

She held out the offending white *kapp*, the strings dangling over the sides of her palm. Bethany had put on her dress and let her braid her hair. And that was as far as she could get her to budge.

Annie wanted to rip off her own *kapp* and pull her hair out. A soft knock at the bedroom door interrupted the stalemate.

"Come in," she called.

Julia opened the door and entered, a smile on her pretty face. Today she was walking around without any stockings or shoes on her feet. For a moment, Annie felt a tug of jealousy. What would it feel like to allow herself to not wear stockings, to allow the scars to show? She remembered Tyler's words, how he had told her she was beautiful, scars and all.

But was she brave enough? Someday, she promised herself. But not yet.

"Can I help you, Julia?" She smiled back at the other women. Her warm brown eyes were filled with kindness and joy. Julia had been busy. Annie could smell the rich aroma of coffee, and the warm smell of biscuits floated in the air. Her stomach rumbled. It was breakfast time. She'd eat as soon as she convinced her daughter to put on the *kapp*.

"I wanted to let you know that breakfast is ready. Ty and Abraham have already gone out to the barn. I believe that they were discussing things that they were needing at the market in town. They might be planning a trip."

Her interest piqued. The market, from all accounts, was a street of small family-owned shops and vendors. It was a popular spot for Amish and non-Amish alike to shop and gather. She'd been wanting to go there herself, just to see it.

She sighed. "That sounds like fun."

Bethany blurted out, "I don't wanna wear the little hat this morning. Kayla wasn't wearing it yesterday."

Julia smiled, a flash of sympathy in her eyes. "Yes, it's true that she wasn't wearing the *kapp* in the house. But she couldn't go outside without wearing it. If you want to eat breakfast without it on, that is fine. You will not be able to go and see Mrs. Feathers without it, though."

Bethany's pout grew less pronounced. She looked outside several times. The lure of the lovely summer weather and the chicken were strong inducements. Annie bit back her smile. She had a feeling the chicken was going to win.

Finally, Bethany raised her big blue eyes to her mother. "Can I eat breakfast without the little hat, Mommy, please? I will put it on before I go see my chicken."

Annie nodded, flashing a grateful smile at Julia. The other woman nodded. Happy again, Bethany ran out of the room, calling Kayla's name.

"Thank you." Annie sighed. "She doesn't understand why we can't go home."

"It's not an easy thing." Julia paused. "You know that I was in witness protection, too?"

Annie nodded.

Julia continued. "My son witnessed a gang shooting." She nodded when Annie gasped and covered her mouth with her hands. "It was terrifying. The gang members were literally in our apartment. We had to hide in a bathroom. When we went into witness protection, I worked as Abraham's housekeeper. He had left the Amish community and married but returned once he was a widower. I know how it feels to be running for your life with children who are resistant to the Amish way of life."

"Did Kayla—"

"Actually, it was William. But he grew to appreciate Abraham and the life we have here. And I thank God every day that he is no longer involved with the wrong people." She sighed. "It's been a while since I have talked about my past. That's one of the harder things about being in the program."

"I know." Annabelle frowned. "I am dreading someone asking me questions about my life before I came here. It's hard, knowing I can never tell anyone outside of the program anything about my real past. I can't talk about my parents or my brother—" Tears filled her eyes as she thought of her family.

"It can be difficult. Remember, though. Everyone inside this house understands what you're going through."

Reflecting on Julia's words, Annabelle walked with her to the kitchen. It was nice to be around people who understood. Just to be on the safe side, she decided she would still refrain from talking about her family. It hurt, knowing that no one would truly know who she was while she was in the program.

Tyler would. She blinked at the thought. No matter how long they were in the program, as long as they were together, she would have one person who knew who she was. One person who would know the past she couldn't talk about. She shrugged away the thought. But as she followed Julia downstairs, her steps were lighter.

The children were already inside the open kitchen. The table was long and wooden, obviously handcrafted. So were the chairs. They had sat to eat. Following the Amish custom, the children and the women bowed their heads to say a silent blessing over their food. Annie still felt odd not praying out loud as she had done at home with Bethany.

The biscuits were light and flaky, absolutely delicious. Especially drizzled with warm honey. The children had just been excused when the men entered the house. Both men took off their wide-brimmed hats and hung them up on the hooks right inside the door. Ty had continued to grow a beard, but no mustache, as a sign that he was a married man, though in name only. Annie had trouble getting used to it. She had known him for over eight years. In that time, he had never worn a beard. Not even a goatee.

"Good morning, Julia. Annie," Ty greeted the women as he sat himself at the table. Abraham joined them shortly, a mug of hot coffee in his hands.

"Ty and I have been planning, isn't that right, Ty?" Abraham's face, which had been rather serious, lightened considerably when creased with a smile, the way it was now.

"Yes, indeed we have." Ty winked at Annie. "We have things we need from the market. What say you, Annie, my girl, to a trip to the market?"

"Could we?" She hadn't meant to squeal, but judging from the grins on the other faces, they didn't mind. She hadn't left the property since they'd arrived. She was beginning to feel a bit closed in. A trip to the market might not be much, but it would get her out of the house for a while. Then her enthusiasm dimmed. "But I'm not sure. I don't know that I want to bring Bethany—"

"Leave her with Kayla, William and I," Julia interrupted. "You need a break, Annie. This would be perfect. And we really do need some items from the market."

She bit her lip. Could they really do it? "But what if we are recognized? I don't want to lead anyone back to you."

Abraham nodded. "We have talked about this. You cannot spend your time imprisoned here. But I understand your concern. Wear your own clothes. That way, if you are recognized, no one will be led here. I will take you in the buggy and drop you off before the market. That way you won't be seen leaving here *Englisch*."

The more she considered the idea, the more excited she became. To leave the farmhouse, to go into town, even if only for an hour, would be wonderful. And she had to admit, if only to herself, she wanted to have some time away with just Tyler. Time where she could explore the idea of whether or not she could allow herself to truly give him another chance.

"Can you wait for fifteen minutes?" She spun to see the smile break across his face like a ray of sunlight.

"I can even give you twenty." He winked, and her stomach fluttered.

She spun again to face Julia. "You don't mind? Really?"

Julia laughed and waved her hands at Annie. "Go. We will watch the child."

She needed no other encouragement. Forgetting to be dignified, she sprinted up the stairs. Moving quickly around the bedroom, she gathered her clothes and changed. She decided to leave her hair up and her *kapp* on for the time being. She didn't want to give herself away to anyone looking inside the buggy.

When Tyler saw her in her normal dress, but with a *kapp* on her head, he smiled so wide the corners of his eyes crinkled. That was a smile she hadn't seen in a long time. She had missed it but didn't realize it until this very moment.

Tyler looked more like himself in his jeans.

"I guess I should wear my hat in the buggy so we match."

She giggled. "I feel like a teenager. This is ridiculous."

His smile faded, but his eyes remained soft. "It's not ridiculous, Annie. You have been a trouper through all of this. You deserve a break."

They both did. She just hoped they could get one.

When was the last time he had heard Annie laugh? It had been too long. He was enjoying the silly mood she was in on the way to the market. The buggy swayed slightly due to an uneven patch in the road. Their shoulders touched. He wished he could stretch his arm across the back of the seat and wrap it around her shoulders.

He didn't think she was ready for that. Actually, he wasn't sure he was ready for it, either. The feelings that were starting to rise were messing with his judgment. The past week had been amazing. The simplicity of the Amish life had allowed them to spend time together as a family without the distractions that normally surrounded them. Even while they were sharing a table with Abraham's family, he could gradually see her relaxing more this week. Bethany had been able to be a kid again, and he had seen the pleasure glowing in Annie's eyes and smile as she had stood watch over the little girl that held both of their hearts in her small hands.

But as much as he enjoyed this respite, he could never quite forget that somewhere, men were searching for him. Because of his job, he was again in a killer's sight. He just didn't know how he'd walk away from her again when this was all over. Being in her presence, day after day, he could feel her inching her way back into his heart.

As the buggy drew closer to town, a conviction grew in his chest. Annie needed to know the truth about what had happened. Every time he saw her wearing stockings when Julia walked around her house barefoot, he was filled with guilt. He knew that he was the reason that she hid her legs.

He could never forget that.

Would she forgive him? He hoped and prayed that she would, but honestly, he didn't know what she would say, or do. He had hurt her so many times in the past, he wondered if this would be the one that would break their connection for good.

The buggy jerked as it halted. They both jolted forward slightly. They had arrived.

Annie carefully removed her *kapp* and set it gently on the seat. She reached up and unpinned her braid so that it swung freely past her shoulders. He took off his hat and set it next to her head covering. Both of them put on baseball caps, pulling them on securely.

Nervously, they exchanged glances. This was it.

Getting out of the buggy, they both cast furtive glances around. No one was about.

"I will pick you up here at two," Abraham said.

"Sounds good. Thanks for the ride."

They watched their friend drive away, then they started toward the market. Without thinking about it, Tyler reached out and grabbed Annie's hand. The moment they touched, he felt her stiffen. Now she would pull away. But she didn't. After a moment, he felt her relax again. He smiled, swinging their hands between them.

They reached the edge of the market. It was bustling with activity. Many of the shops had brought some of their merchandise outside and set up displays on the sidewalks. Amish and *Englisch* alike mingled in the warm June morning. It was going to be hot by the time noon rolled around, but right at the moment the weather was warm with a light breeze.

Tyler flicked his gaze over to Annie. He grinned. She was looking everywhere she could, her eyes wide as she took in everything. He had known she'd react this way. Annie loved seeing new places and watching people. To her, this was more fun than any fancy restaurant or going to a show. He'd missed that in his life these past few years.

They wandered around to the different shops. Tyler didn't buy anything. Whatever they bought, they'd have to carry with them. Knowing that someone was after them and might show up at any moment meant that they had to be ready to run and could not be hampered with nonessential items. Abraham would be purchasing whatever was needed back at the farm. Anything else was just a useless material possession. Not worth the trouble.

At lunchtime, they grabbed hot dogs and sodas at one of the food stands that dotted the sidewalk.

Every now and then, he looked around. He could never get over the feeling that disaster was about to strike. Maybe coming to the market had not been a good idea, after all. He had done it to get Annie away from the farm, knowing that it would please her. Now he felt like they were wearing targets on their backs.

He looked at his watch. It was one thirty. They had half an hour to go before they were to meet up with Abraham again. Although they had enjoyed their outing, he felt like he would be glad to get back to the Beiler home.

He was probably being foolish. Still, he remained on alert.

A few minutes later, he was glad that he had not completely let down his guard.

"Ty." Annie nudged his side with her elbow, her voice a tense whisper. "We're being watched."

His pulse hiked. She was staring off to the left a bit, her brow wrinkled. He noted that she was tugging at her braid. Although she looked calm enough to the casual observer, the increased pressure on his hand told him clearly that she was becoming agitated.

Stay calm. Look casual. Pulling her closer, he pretended to kiss her head, angling his face so he could peer over her. A young man with cold dark eyes was staring straight at them, his gaze narrowed. It was a calculated gaze. The stare of a man trying to figure something out.

Or maybe he was trying to imagine what Tyler looked like without his slight beard.

"Turn away," he whispered out of the corner of his mouth. "Pretend nothing is wrong.

Like we are just any other couple here to look at the shops. We are just going to casually walk away. Stay close. We may need to run."

She nodded and turned with him.

They didn't talk. His ears were hyperfocused now, listening for any sign that they had been recognized. They skirted their way past two buildings successfully.

"We'll just wander around the side of that next building," he decided. "Then we will have to run. Do you—"

Whatever he was going to ask was forgotten.

"Tyler!" a voice yelled behind him.

Instinctively, he whipped his head in the direction of the voice. Screams followed as the man dropped the fliers and pulled out a gun.

"Run!"

Annie didn't need the urging. They bolted. Tearing past the shops, they both kept as close to walls as they could. They cleared the store and tore up the hill. A shot rang out. Then another. Metal clanged. Something dropped behind them. Right where they had been.

They couldn't stop to look.

Tyler tugged Annie toward another group of buildings.

"No!" Annie gasped. "Too many people!"

She was right. The man chasing them probably wouldn't care if he hit someone else.

They darted behind an empty tourist bus that was parked along the side of the road. Tyler peeked out, keeping himself low. The man who had been chasing them was still there, but he seemed to have lost them in the crowd.

That wouldn't last for long. Sooner or later, he would head their way. Then what? When the man paused to turn and search, Tyler waited until he was turned in the opposite direction. Then he pulled Annie out from behind the bus and into the building that the bus was parked in front of. It was a large auction house. There were rows upon rows of vendors set up inside with their crafts and wares. And there was a door out the other side.

Sirens shrieked and drew closer. Tyler could have wilted where he stood in relief. Still, he wasn't going to let down his guard. Even if the police were on the scene, he couldn't assume that the danger following them was over.

They hurried through the building at a swift walk, trying not to be too conspicuous. The noise level in the place was over the top. Tyler kept looking back. No sign of the man.

They made it to the other side of the building without anyone calling out to them.

A few seconds later, the sounds of gunfire could be heard in the background. He heard people screaming. Someone—no doubt an officer—shouted for people to get down.

Tyler's mouth was dry. He put his hand against Annie's back, silently encouraging her to walk in front of him. If bullets went flying toward them again, he wanted to keep her from being hit.

There was a path leading away from the building. It was convenient. But far too visible. Tyler pulled Annie off the path. A smaller building, probably for storage, was off to the side. He pulled them behind it. The good thing was that no one could see them there. Of course, that meant that they would not be able to see anyone coming, either. It was a chance he had to take.

The shouting and the gunfire behind them stopped. He wished he could go back and check it out, to be sure. That was a chance he couldn't take, though.

They needed to regroup and consider their options.

"We have twenty minutes until Abraham comes for us."

He heard Annie's breathing. There was a small gasp. Annie was in pain.

"I think I've been shot."

TWELVE

Shot?

Feeling like he was moving in slow motion, Tyler pivoted to face his wife.

Her face was pale and pinched with pain. His chest tightened as he looked over her. Then his glance fell on the gravel at their feet. It was a mixture of various shades of white and gray. There were some almost black patches.

And every few inches, a splotch of red.

Blood.

His wife, his Annie, had been shot.

Feelings of remorse and self-recrimination threatened to overwhelm him, but he shoved them aside. He didn't have time for that.

He couldn't see where she was bleeding from.

"Where, Annie?" His voice came out harsh with fear.

"My leg."

He could see it then. Her right lower leg. There was a hole. A dark circular stain was slowly growing, creeping out across the faded denim of her blue jeans.

He had to stop the bleeding. But with what? He had nothing on him that would be useful. He had to go and find something. He clenched his teeth and peeked around the corner of the shed. No one was coming toward them. He had to take a chance, although he hated to leave her by herself. She'd be safer here than coming with him, though.

"Wait here."

She protested, but he was too focused to stop. Running back inside the auction building, he let his eyes adjust to the sudden dim light after being out in the blinding sunlight. No sign of the man who had shot at them. Quickly, Tyler purchased two bottles of water and a T-shirt. He didn't even stop to look at the design.

Picking up his purchases, he hurried back to Annie. She was right where he had left her, sitting behind the shed with her back up against the brown wall. Her legs were stretched out in front of her.

Kneeling at her side, he slowly began to inch up her jeans toward her knee to expose the wound.

"Wait," she cried, a thin thread of panic running through her voice.

He frowned. "Annie. I don't want to hurt you, but I have to stop the bleeding."

He met her gaze. He didn't like the resigned look that entered her eyes. Her lips tightened, meshing together to form a straight line. After a few eternal seconds, she nodded.

That was all he needed. He resumed his task. Thankfully, she had chosen to wear looser-fitting jeans this morning. If she had opted for skinny jeans, he would have had to have cut them. And he didn't have anything on him to do that. Finally, he could see the wound. He let out the breath he was holding. It was not as bad as he had feared. More of a graze than a full-on hit. He would not have to worry about a bullet still in the leg. He opened one of the waters and poured it gently over the wound. Taking the T-shirt, he patted the wound. More blood welled. He would need to put pressure on it. Placing his left hand on her leg to hold it steady, he held the shirt against the bleeding side of her calf with his right hand. He felt her flinch once. She trembled. He winced. He had to be hurting her. It couldn't be helped, although he wished it had been him and not her who had been wounded.

"Are you okay?"

Her face was turned away from him. She nodded, but didn't say anything.

He checked the wound several times. After about ten minutes, he was satisfied that the bleeding had stopped. He gripped the shirt at a seam and pulled. After a second, he heard the gratifying sound of fabric ripping. He kept pulling. He ripped until he had enough material to make a bandage, one that could be hopefully covered by her pant leg.

"I think that's good. Do you think you can walk on that?" Tyler pulled the pant leg back down, completely covering the emergency bandage, and slid his gaze up to her face. To his astonishment, tears were streaking down her face. "Annie! Did I hurt you? I'm so sorry. I tried to be as gentle as I could."

She shuddered. "It's not that." The words sounded like she half swallowed them. She gulped.

He was confused. "If I didn't hurt you, why are you crying?"

It could have been a reaction to the stress, but he didn't think so. Her eyes, even though tear-filled, were luminous, staring at him almost with awe. That was not a sight he was used to seeing.

"You touched them." The whisper was soft.

Huh?

"What?"

"My scars. You put your hand right over them as if you didn't even see them."

Oh. He so didn't want to have this conversation sitting here, vulnerable. They needed to get moving.

"I didn't see them. Annie, they have never bothered me like they do you. Look, I need to tell you something, but we need to get walking first. We can't be sitting here. We're too out in the open."

She nodded once, then held out her hand for him to assist her to stand. She braced herself against him and let her weight gradually fall on her injured leg. "I can walk."

Keeping to the edge of the woods, they circled the street where the market was set up, deliberately going the extra block so as not to lose the cover the trees gave them. Several times, they stopped to give Annie's leg a chance to rest. It was a painstakingly slow journey.

"We should call Karl," Tyler said.

"Oh, yes." Annie stopped, and searched through her purse for the phone that the marshal had left with her. "Here, you talk to him. I'm going to sit down for a few minutes."

Quickly, he called Karl and left a voice mail when the marshal didn't answer.

Tyler turned and watched Annie with concern. Something was going on in her complicated mind. It had something to do with her scars. He had always known that she felt they were ugly. And he had tried to convince her that they weren't as bad as she thought. But maybe there was more to it than that. Something deeper.

He remembered something his old pastor had said after his mother had lost hope and died soon after his father was gone. *Not all scars show up on the skin. Some are soul-deep.*

Was this one of those cases? He remembered how embarrassed she was to let him see her scars, even though he had seen them before. And he remembered her reaction when he had touched them. Did she think that the scars were what drove him to withdraw? He had kept silent to protect his family, but had his silence also led to his wife's loss of self-confidence? It was years too late, and maybe his timing was off, but he needed to let her know the truth. If something happened to him, he didn't want Annie to continue believing a lie.

Even if she despised him for the truth.

* * *

It didn't take long before Annie's leg was throbbing intensely. Every step shot pain up her leg. She didn't complain. She didn't want to appear weak. But there was no way she could keep herself from limping. What if she had to go to the hospital? Would Karl put a guard outside her door?

Suddenly a thought occurred to her. What if the man who had shot her had escaped the police? Did he know that he hit her? *What if he searches the hospitals?*

Her breathing quickened. The only place she would feel safe was back at the Beiler farm. She nearly cried when they finally found Abraham. The buggy might have appeared more fragile than a car, but to her, it was beautiful and a sign of God's grace and protection.

For his part, Abraham looked like he had been pacing back and forth. There was a frantic look about his eyes. It was a bit startling. He looked like such a calm fellow. So strong and quiet. Seeing him so obviously on edge was odd.

He and Julia had been part of the program, though. Which meant that he knew all the dangers that went along with it. Not to mention, she reminded herself, he had been a cop for ten years.

Relief flashed across the older man's face when he saw them racing, or in her case limping, toward him. He frowned as he watched her approach.

"What happened?" Abraham asked the moment they appeared. "Two police cars passed me on the way. When I arrived, people walked by me talking about someone shooting at the police in the market."

Tyler scanned the area, his mouth grim. "Let me tell you when we get back to your house. I don't think it's safe here. The sooner we can leave, the better."

Abraham didn't ask any more questions. He hopped up on the seat. The moment that Tyler and Annie were settled in the buggy, he flicked the reins and clicked his tongue, and the horse started forward.

Annie and Tyler quickly put their headwear back on. They sat side by side, the tension vibrating off both of them. Tyler reached over and grabbed hold of her hand. She not only let him hold it, but she also squeezed his and kept a tight grip on it, as if she was concerned that he would be ripped away from her.

Annie couldn't stop shaking. "What if the

police didn't get him? He could still be out there, watching."

Tyler nodded. Letting go of her hand for a moment, he reached down and pulled a light-weight blanket over them. "Get down."

They both sank below the thin blanket. Soon, Annie felt sweat beginning to trickle down her neck. It was a toss-up whether it was more from the heat or the fear.

The moment they reached the house, Tyler helped her inside. "We need to check your leg. I am worried that it might get infected."

She was too tired to argue. She changed back into her Amish dress, knowing that it would be easier for him to see to her leg without her jeans getting in the way. This time, when he looked at her leg, she didn't feel the embarrassment that she did earlier. She was still touchy about the scars, but he'd already seen them and hadn't acted like they repulsed him.

She had to rethink a lot of things she'd thought over the years. The idea made her squirm. As much as he had done or not done in their marriage, had she made the mistake of being overly judgmental toward him?

The idea bothered her. A lot. She had always considered herself a forgiving and merciful person. But now she wondered if she had withheld those qualities from the one person in her life she had vowed to show them to.

Julia came to assist before Annie could get too far into her own examination of conscience. She brought clean bandages and some antibacterial ointment. "We can have the doctor out tomorrow if it starts to look infected. Right now, it looks sore, but it really is not that much more than a skin wound."

Annie sank back against the chair, relieved. Tyler did not look convinced. "Ty, let's leave it until the morning."

Reluctantly, he nodded.

He was still looking pensive. Something else was on his mind.

"What's up?"

"I need to talk with you," he muttered. Julia and Abraham melted away. Julia said, "William has the girls. I will tell him to keep them out until you're done."

When they were alone, they looked at each other. Annie waited for him to break the silence.

Finally, he sighed. "I have a confession to make. I'm not sure if you will hate me or not when I'm done. At least, more than you do already."

She cringed. "I don't hate you, Ty. I never did. I was hurt and confused."

He looked off in the distance. It was as if he didn't even hear her. He seemed to be lost in his own memories.

"I don't think I ever really told you what happened with my father." He looked down, rubbing the toe of his shoe against some imaginary piece of dirt. "I know that you were aware that he had died when I was fifteen, but there was more to it than that. You see, my dad was a good man. He tended to believe the best about everyone. Even when they didn't deserve it."

She could already tell that this was going to be a story that broke her heart. She would hear the story through, though—she could tell that Tyler needed to tell her.

Tyler seem to have trouble finding the words to say what happened. She tried to help him along.

"Did someone take advantage of your dad?"

He nodded. "My uncle—his brother. He had gotten into it with some very bad people. When my dad tried to help him by going to the cops, those people decided to try and ruin him. And they did."

Her hand went to her throat—she was horrified.

Tyler continued his story. "My parents went

to the police again. By this time, they had lost almost everything. And I don't just mean material things. They had lost their self-respect. Friends had stopped calling. My best friend's parents even told him that he couldn't hang out with me anymore. Unfortunately, my parents couldn't afford a good lawyer. And the court-appointed one just didn't seem to be taking the case seriously. So no one was ever punished except for my dad and my mom."

He caught her eyes with his, and the breath stuck in her throat. The pain she saw reached out and grabbed her.

"It killed him." His voice was so low, she had to lean forward to hear him clearly. "Oh, I know it was officially a heart attack, but this tragedy is what killed my dad. And it broke my mother's heart and she died, too. When I was offered a scholarship, I knew that I wanted to be a lawyer. I wanted to put people like that in jail. I took great pleasure in putting them in jail, too."

His head dropped into his hands. "And that's when my trouble started. I became so obsessed with putting the bad guys in jail, that I neglected you. Eventually, though, I paid for my arrogance. One of the men I put behind bars had a son. A son who promised to make me pay. I could never prove it, but a week later, a truck ran through a light and into our living room window."

Her heart stopped. The accident. Her scars. They led back to Tyler and his job.

Annabelle didn't know what to think. Or how to feel. To know that the accident that had caused her so much misery and pain was, in fact, no accident at all. If she could believe Tyler.

And she did.

It all made sense now. The way he'd started to pull back after her accident. The way he had suddenly not wanted the family to go anywhere.

"That's why you didn't go to my father's funeral." It wasn't a question.

He nodded. "I never wanted to hurt you. I was afraid that if I showed up, he would go after your family. I was terrified that you or Bethany would be hurt or killed. I knew that my job was a danger to you. The man who wanted me to pay died of a heart attack. Then, two days later, you walked out. When you left, I wanted to go after you. But I knew it was for the best. I had many enemies. I couldn't guarantee another wouldn't have come after me."

"I can't believe you didn't let me know what was happening!" She shook her head.

"And what if we were in danger because you weren't there to protect us?"

Tyler sighed and dropped his head into his hands. "I made sure that people knew we were not together in any sense. I stayed away from Bethany so it would appear that I was an uninterested father. And I have a friend who is a detective. He checked up on you now and then. I did whatever I could to make sure you were safe. I was pretty sure that the danger had been eradicated, but I couldn't risk it."

Annabelle felt like she was watching some poorly written soap opera. Any moment now, something would pop out of nowhere to save them. But, of course, it would not. "I thought that you were pulling back because my scars disgusted you."

Had she really just told him that? She was a bit embarrassed by her vanity.

His shocked face told her more than his words could that the thought had never entered his mind. "Annie, you're beautiful. You always have been. I thought your scars were beautiful, too."

She ducked her head. That was hard to believe.

"It's true. Every time I saw your scars, I remembered running to find you and lifting your lifeless body in my arms. I thought you were dead. I looked at your scars, and I remembered the gratitude I felt at knowing that you were alive."

Their conversation was interrupted when Abraham entered the room carrying a cell phone. She recognized it as the same kind of phone that Karl had given her and Tyler.

"Is it Karl?" Tyler asked, accepting the phone when Abraham held it out to him.

"Yes."

When Tyler answered the phone, she knew that their conversation was over. Frowning, she rapped her knuckles against the side of the chair. Her stomach was unsettled. Partly from the conversation they had just had, and partly from the events of the day. She remembered how gentle Tyler had been as he had seen to her wound. She had been so angry with him for so long, she had forgotten how sweet he could be.

Was she still angry with him? Now that she had an explanation, she understood what had happened between them. If she was honest with herself, she probably had let her insecurities caused by her scars keep her from fighting for their marriage.

Tyler had pushed them away to protect

them. She got that. She even could respect it, although she felt he was wrong.

What she didn't know was whether she could ever trust him not to do the same thing in the future if they were in danger.

THIRTEEN

The doctor came out to see her the next day. He cleaned her wound with a solemn expression and then told her that the next time she helped clean her husband's hunting rifle, they needed to make sure it was not loaded first. Blinking, she agreed. Cleaning a hunting rifle? She probably couldn't tell him that someone had shot at her.

Tyler and Abraham had gone to the barn to work by the time the doctor had finished and left. Sighing, she realized that there would not be an opportunity to talk with him more about what had happened in the past until later.

Did she want to talk more? Because if she didn't talk to him, then she didn't need to deal with the emotional bulldozer he had hit her with the day before.

Did she blame him for her accident? Could

she allow their relationship to continue to grow, knowing what she knew?

It was fine while they were here, hidden in Amish country. But what happened when they returned home, if they returned home? She knew that he regretted missing out on their lives. She also believed that he did what he could to protect them.

What she didn't know, and what she had been afraid to ask, was whether or not he would make the same choices again. Would he, if they returned to their lives, again bury himself in his work at the price of their family?

He had felt driven by what happened to his father. She got that. But she could not go through the emotional wringer he had put them through again.

A car drove into the driveway. It was Karl. She moved toward the door to let him in, but Julia beat her there.

"Karl!" The Amish woman greeted him with a smile. "I did not expect to see you again so soon. Although, you are always welcome."

"Good morning, Julia. I didn't plan on visiting so soon." His gaze found Annie. "Ty said you had been attacked and that you had been shot."

She nodded. "That is true. I don't think it's serious, though."

"The whole situation is serious. I need to talk with you both."

"He's working with Abraham in the barn. I'll go get him." Julia hurried off. Less than ten minutes later, she returned, Tyler striding in behind her.

"Karl!" The men shook hands.

"Ty. As I was telling Annie, your situation is serious, but I do have some good news. Someone had heard gunshots and had called the police to the market. When they arrived and surrounded him, the man refused to surrender and began shooting at the police. They returned fire, and the man in question was killed. Although I never take someone's death lightly, I am relieved that he never had a chance to reveal that he had seen you."

"How do you know that?" She clenched her fists tight enough for her short nails to dig into her palms.

"The police identified him as someone local. He had a long rap sheet, mostly minor crimes. His computer and his phone have been checked out. He apparently got word of the bounty on your head. As far as we can tell, he was at the market and recognized you from the pictures that had been circulated."

"It seems odd that he would recognize us." Tyler narrowed his eyes, his lips tight.

"Not really. This guy was known for his memory. What we used to call a photographic memory. The fact that he recognized you isn't odd, but it isn't exactly something most people can do, either. He made no phone calls after he saw you. Were you dressed Amish?"

"No, and we didn't arrive at the market in the buggy. Abraham dropped us off before we got there."

"Good. That should help." He frowned. "I think you should still be safe here. This scenario could have happened anywhere we placed you. But I am going to start planning for a new placement for you. Just in case we need to move quick."

Her heart sank. She had just started to get comfortable with the Beilers. And Bethany would be difficult. The only reason her daughter really tolerated their situation was because of Kayla and her chicken. She knew that her daughter was becoming anxious to return home. He hadn't said they had to move, though. Only that it was a possibility.

Unwillingly, her eyes moved to Tyler. He had been quick-thinking during their ordeal. Had he always been that competent in dealing with a crisis? She was discovering new depths to him.

Karl continued. "For now, your cover is safe. I just would ask that you avoid the market until things settle down."

He glanced around. "Are the kids here?"

"William took them out to the neighbors'. New kittens."

"Ah. Well, that sounds great. I want to talk with Abraham as long as I'm here."

Disappointment settled over her. She had enjoyed the market. Well, until the man started shooting. Knowing that she would not be able to go again anytime soon made her feel like the prison bars were coming in tighter.

"I'll show you where he is," Tyler said. "He was going out in the woods to check on something."

Karl walked outside with Tyler. Annie sighed, discouraged.

"Annie, it will work out."

Annie slowly rotated on her stockinged feet to face Julia. "I'm not sure it will. I feel like everything is coming unglued. Things I have known for years are not as they seem. My husband has someone after him, and therefore us, and now I can't even go into the market."

She needed to stop talking because she

sounded like a teenager. Any moment she'd say, "It's not fair!"

"Come, sit." Julia brought two coffee mugs to the table. She joined her. "Have you talked with Ty about how you are feeling?"

A flush crawled up her neck and into her cheeks. "No. Julia, Ty and I, well, we're married. But we have been living separate lives for several years now. I had always believed it was because he chose his job over us. Now, I'm not sure what to think."

Briefly, she outlined what Tyler had told her, skipping over the part about his father. When she told the other woman about the accident that had nearly killed her and had left her with so many emotional and physical scars, Julia covered her mouth with her hand.

"Oh, that is so terrible!"

Annie realized there were tears on her cheeks. She dashed them away angrily. She was crying way too much lately.

"I don't know what to do. I am afraid of the fact that we seem to be growing so close. I don't want to get hurt again." She wasn't worried about him abandoning Bethany again, though. He'd said he wouldn't, and despite everything that had happened in the past, she trusted him to keep his word.

Julia considered. "Sometimes life is hard.

Before I met Abraham, I was struggling to raise two children alone. William, he's such a wonderful young man. And he is such a joy to me. Now. A year ago, though, he was in trouble. Well, you remember what I told you, about him getting involved with a gang. He even ran away."

"No!" Shocked, Annie stared at her new friend.

"It is true. Abraham, his story was equally harsh. His first wife and child were murdered, killed by a car bomb. I do not know how he survived that."

Neither did she. The thought of anything happening to Bethany turned her stomach. How did one pick up the pieces after such devastating events?

She asked the question out loud.

"The only way I know to survive is through my faith."

Annie bit her lip. "I'm afraid I haven't relied on God as much as I should through this. I tend to leap and think of going to God afterward."

A brief smile flickered across Julia's face. "That is human nature. But I think the more we trust in Him, the more resilient we will be when the hard times come. Because they will come. Having faith does not mean we have an easy path."

The truth of the statement hit her. She had acted as if things should be easy, because she had faith. When she left Tyler, she had expected him to come after her, and then pouted when he hadn't.

And despite his distancing himself from them, he wasn't the one who left.

That was all on her.

Karl excused himself to take a phone call, leaving Tyler and Abraham alone. As they usually did, they began to talk and debate current issues. Abraham Beiler was one of the most interesting men that Tyler had ever met. The man had lived a very hard life, and had managed not only to survive, but also to thrive. Tyler shuddered even to think about losing his family so violently.

The one thing that made Tyler uncomfortable was how unreserved Abraham was when it came to talking about his faith. Tyler realized he had kind of given up on his faith when things had turned sour. He hadn't even given God a chance to work before he had pushed Him out of his life. Instead, he had just accepted things as they were. His life stalled.

When was the last time he had a real friend

to talk to? Even when he was supposedly happily married to Annie, on some level he always kept his emotional distance from her. It was almost like he had always known that one day she would leave him.

No, that wasn't true. Her leaving had shocked him. But what had shocked him even more was that he hadn't really even noticed how far apart they'd gotten. He hadn't noticed how much pain she was in. Was it by choice?

"Ty, how is Annie feeling today?" Abraham asked. It was almost as if he knew whom Tyler was thinking so hard about.

"Oh, I think she's doing all right. She's strong." He paused, then blurted out, "I hate that she was hurt because of me."

Now what on earth had made him say that? Abraham was going to think he was off his rocker. That's not the sort of conversation one has with a virtual stranger.

Except, Abraham and Julia didn't really feel like strangers. It was probably because Tyler knew that they were in the witness protection program, as well. And lived to tell about it. Abraham had told him about the deaths of his wife and child, as well as the gang members who had been hunting down William. Now, they were a family, living a simple life far from where they had started out.

That made him pause again. The Beiler family was still in the witness protection program. And they probably always would be.

What if he and Annie were always in the program, too? They couldn't go on as they were. Deep inside, he knew that he still had feelings for her. They had never really died out. He had just shoved them aside so that he could carry on doing his job. A job, if he was honest, he had come to despise. He felt no joy inside when he was working. Only a sense of never-ending duty.

Could they be a couple again? But what would happen if they left the program? He didn't know if he even wanted to go there.

Abraham was staring at him, an expectant look on his face. He was no doubt waiting for Tyler to explain why he had been avoiding his wife. Tyler laughed to himself, although there was no humor in the sound. He'd been doing a lot of explaining himself lately. He wasn't exactly sure that he enjoyed that.

"Hey, Ty! Abraham!" Tyler was grateful to see Karl approaching. "I have some news for you."

Tyler was glad to know that the man who'd been shooting at them hadn't found out where they were.

But Annie wouldn't be happy about having to stay away from the market. He knew that she had enjoyed the experience, minus the shooting, of course.

"What I really wanted to tell you," Karl said, his tone catching Tyler's attention, "is that the judge has moved up the trial date. And Billy Clarke, our resident technology whiz kid, has stumbled on information that the bounty out on you has increased. Tyler, I don't need to tell you that you and Annie have to stay under the radar. Now, more than ever. Every bounty hunter and petty thief in the continental US will be after you. They won't care if they bring you in dead or alive."

Karl stayed through dinner, then he departed with a final warning for them to be careful and to stay alert. After he left, Tyler asked Annie to take a walk outside with him. Her eyes widened. He'd caught her by surprise. She said yes, to his relief.

They stepped outside and moved away from the house. Not too far away. Just far enough away where their conversation would not carry through the windows to the people still inside. As they walked, he laced his fingers through hers.

"Annie..." He couldn't bring himself to look at her. Not yet. "Karl brought some news today."

She halted and tugged him to a stop with her. "Is it about the man who shot me? I know that Karl said that he doesn't think our cover has been blown."

"Yes, and no." He caught her other hand and leaned toward her. Their foreheads touched. *Just for a moment*, he thought, *let me pretend that she still loves me and that everything will be fine.* "You already know that he's no longer a threat. What Karl just told me is that the trial date has been moved up."

Annie pulled back. He managed to mask his disappointment. "That's good, right? The sooner the trial ends, the sooner people will stop chasing us."

"Not if the bounty is still there. Some people will do anything to make money." Reluctantly, he released her hands and took a step back. Immediately, he wanted to grab them again.

He heard her harsh breath.

"Karl thinks that the number of people out to get me has increased. Exponentially."

She was silent for a minute. He waited.

"Will we ever be safe? Or will we have to stay in witness protection forever?"

He wished he knew the answer to that question.

FOURTEEN

"Annie!" Tyler walked toward her, waving something.

Wait. Was that the newspaper? She grinned as she grabbed at it. Julia and Abraham read the local Amish newspaper, but they didn't get the *Englisch* one on a daily basis. She missed reading the comics.

"When did you get this?" She held the paper close to her as she stared up at him. My, he looked pleased with himself.

"I remembered how you enjoyed reading the comics, so I asked Abraham if he could pick up a newspaper while he was in town."

"Oh, thank you!" Stretching up, she planted a kiss on his cheek. Their eyes met. Unwilling to decipher the emotions flashing in his eyes, or flooding her system, she took the paper and escaped to her room, feeling his eyes following her.

She flipped through until she found the

comics. They were as funny as she remembered. Maybe even more so because she had not had access to them.

She flipped the page again. And froze, bile rising in her throat. A picture of a block where three houses had been decimated by fire was in the center of the page. Her mother's house was one of the three destroyed! She would not have known it if it was not for the undamaged houses surrounding the destroyed buildings.

Feverishly, she read the rest of the article. No mention of people dead, although the article did mention several injuries. Her hand went to her throat. Swallowing hard, she forced herself to read on, blinking back the tears. The local police believed that the fires might have been started by a serial arsonist, one that had hit houses in several states. That was probably why it made the paper in Ohio. Normally, fires in Southern Illinois wouldn't be reported this far east.

Her mother had gone to stay with Ethan. She wasn't even there. Annabelle kept telling herself that she was being silly.

It didn't matter. No matter how much Annabelle tried to convince herself that her mother was safe and had not been inside the house at the time of the fire, every time she looked at the newspaper and saw the charred remains of her childhood home, a chill went down her spine.

A new thought occurred to her. Her mother had been very resistant to the idea of going to stay with her son. What if, despite all of Ethan's persuasion, her mother had remained stubborn? Ethan would have had no method by which to contact her. What if her mother had been inside when the house had gone up in flames? Images of her mother wounded and lying in a hospital bed tormented her.

She could not endure not knowing the truth!

Annabelle read the article again. All it said was that it was a house owned by a widow in her late sixties. It did not mention anything about anyone being inside the house when it caught fire.

There was no doubt in Annabelle's mind that the police were wrong. This was not the work of a serial arsonist. No, this was the work of someone who was searching for Tyler and her. Someone who didn't know where they were, but who hoped that she would see the news coverage on the fire.

They're just trying to draw us out. She knew that. Deep in her bones, she under-stood that attacking her mother was just a way of getting at her and Tyler. But no matter how much she tried to convince herself that it would be foolish to contact her mother, she could not get that house out of her mind.

She stewed about it all day long. Several times, Tyler asked if she was all right. Even when she said she was, she could tell that he wasn't convinced.

I should show him the article.

But she didn't. She knew that if she showed him the article, Tyler would know that she was thinking of contacting her mother. He would also, most likely, put the blame upon himself. He held himself responsible for way too much as it was.

Wait a minute. She didn't have to contact her mother. Although she very much wanted to be the one to contact her mother. She needed to hear her mother's voice. But she also knew the rules. She could not contact her mother. But she had the phone that the marshals had given her so that she could contact them.

She could contact Karl or Jonathan.

At the first opportunity, Annabelle excused herself to go upstairs to her room. It was after suppertime, but due to the extended summer daylight, she still had plenty of light in her room. She took the cell phone out of her bag and dialed Karl's number with fingers that shook. Now that she was actually taking steps to find out the truth, she was terrified of what she might discover.

The phone rang once. Twice. After four rings, it went to voice mail. She should leave a message. She knew he was busy and would call her back.

She didn't. Instead, she ended the call, knowing that she wouldn't have been able to stand it any longer. She couldn't call from the house phone. That was too risky. Abraham and Tyler were working in the barn. They wouldn't be back for another few hours. Kayla and Bethany were at a neighbor's house. What should she do?

"Annie?" She quickly hid the phone as she heard Julia calling.

Opening her door, she met the other woman in the hall.

"Ah, there you are!" Julia flashed her a warm smile. Annie smiled back, hoping her smile wasn't as wobbly as it felt. "I was thinking about going to the quilt shop for a few supplies. It's not as elegant as going into town, but maybe you would want to go with me?"

"Absolutely!" She jumped at the opportunity. If she found someone with a cell phone, maybe she could make the call. That way, she wouldn't have to conceal a phone on her person.

When they arrived at the quilt shop, her heart sank. The only person present besides Julia and herself was the woman running the store. They got into a lengthy discussion regarding patterns. Bored, Annabelle wandered outside. She started walking around the building, when a van pulled up. Two women and five children spilled from the van, all chattering in loud voices. She winced. She'd gotten used to the quiet manner of Julia.

Seeing her chance, she approached the woman on the far side of the van and asked if she could use her phone. The woman stopped talking and stared at her, her mouth dropping open. Flushing, Annabelle explained that a non-Amish friend's house had burned down and she wanted to check on her. Softening, the woman held out her phone.

"Of course."

Thanking the woman, Annabelle walked a bit apart. For privacy, but also so that Julia would not see her through the window.

She was making a mistake. She needed to wait. But her fingers were already dialing the familiar cell phone number. She held her breath. There was still time to hang up. Her mother would not even recognize the number.

She didn't, though. She was too close to give up.

Clenching her fists, Annabelle waited for her mother to answer her phone.

Come on, Mom. Answer the phone. Come on. She pounded her fist lightly against her thigh as she waited. Every second she grew more tense, trying to keep the thoughts of why her mom might not be answering from creeping into her mind. Finally, after what seemed an eternity, her mother picked up the phone.

"Hello?" Her mother sounded annoyed. Ah! She probably thought it was a telemarketer. Her mother could never be convinced that it wasn't rude to ignore calls from unfamiliar numbers. For once, she was glad.

Annabelle tried to answer her mom but found herself choking up too much.

"Hello?" Now her mom sounded angry.

"Mom!" she blurted out. "Are you all right?"

Just the mere sound of her mother's voice was enough to bring the tears spurting to her eyes. She sniffed and did her best to blink them back. She never cried. For years, she had prided herself on her strength. On her ability to handle anything. Now, it seemed all she ever did was cry.

"Annabelle? Is that you?" There were tears in her mother's voice, as well. "Oh, honey! I am so glad to hear your voice!"

"Mom, I saw the newspaper article. Your house! I was so scared. I was afraid that you were in it. They were saying it might not have been an accident." She had to sit down. She sank down on the bench outside the store. The emotional roller-coaster ride she had been on for the past week was getting to be too much.

"Honey, I'm fine. It's just a house. No one was inside of it. I did what you asked and I'm staying with your brother. We both know that my house did not accidentally go up in flames."

"It had to have been arson." Annie had never been as sure of anything in her life. "Mom, you know that they were out to get me. Hoping I would come home to see you."

"That's what we think, as well. Whatever you do, do not come home. I want to see you, you know that. I think, though, that one of the people trying to find you will be watching me and your brother, hoping to get you. And through you, Tyler." Her mom's voice held no blame. Annie knew that her mother held no rancor against her son-in-law. In fact, she had often told Annie that she prayed that somehow they would get back together someday. Until recently, Annie had thought the idea was ludicrous.

There was a pause on the other end of the phone. When her mother spoke again her voice was softer, smaller somehow. Annie knew that she was not the only one feeling the effects of the separation. "Annabelle, how are you doing? And how is my granddaughter? I have been praying so hard for you. I feel like part of my heart has been ripped apart."

Annie took a deep breath to steady herself. "I know. But we're safe."

Julia would be out any second.

"Mom, I gotta go. Love you."

"Okay, baby girl. Be safe." Her mom hung up the phone.

Annie smiled. Then she frowned. What was that click?

Uneasy, she disconnected the call and returned it to the woman, thanking her for her understanding. Julia came out as they were talking. Fortunately, she didn't appear to have seen what Annabelle had done. That didn't make her feel less guilty for breaking the rules.

She had thought that she would be at peace once she talked with her mother. She did feel better, knowing that her mother was safe. Worry continued to eat at her, niggling itself into her mind long after she went to bed.

She knew that the marshals had good reason to tell clients not to contact people from their past. Her call could get them kicked out of the program. Karl and Jonathan had clearly explained the rules.

And she had deliberately disobeyed them.

Had she just betrayed Tyler?

They had been living with the Beilers for three weeks. Every morning, Tyler woke up wondering if today would be the day that they were discovered. The day that all of their attempts to hide failed.

Whatever happened today, it would be a new experience for them. For the first time, Tyler, Annie and Bethany would be joining the Beiler family at church. He would be meeting the other nineteen families in the district. That was a whole bunch of people who didn't know that they weren't really planning on becoming Amish.

Of course, they might not have a choice.

He shrugged away the thought.

Annie, however, was almost dancing with her excitement. She was so thrilled to finally be meeting more people and getting the chance to get out and be social. Tyler could not help the smile that came to his face as he watched her. She had been so tense lately. Not that he could blame her. It was difficult knowing that people were searching for them. For the first time in days, though, he could see her natural exuberance.

Tyler had helped the men unload the church benches from the wagon. The men had accepted him as part of their group, although some of them had ribbed him about choosing to join the church at such an old age. He scoffed. Old. Yeah, right.

He actually enjoyed being part of the group that set the benches up.

The church service was interesting. It had been so long since he had been to church. He expected to be uncomfortable. And he did squirm a bit. But he was busy experiencing all the new and unexpected differences. Oh sure, he had known from what Abraham had told him that the women and the men would be seated separately. What he hadn't expected was to connect so much with what the bishop was saying. Part of him wondered if the bishop was giving his message for the sake of Annie and Tyler. Tyler remembered that the bishop knew who they were. The bishop's message centered around trusting God even when they were in the desert.

An apt description.

After the service, there was the meal that the community took together. Again, the men and women were seated separately.

For some reason, Tyler was uneasy. He liked being able to see exactly where his wife and daughter were. At the moment, though, they were here surrounded by other people. He really just needed to relax and enjoy the day.

As the men were gathering outside after they had eaten, Tyler overheard a group of the boys talking about a couple of men in town.

Tyler didn't pay too much attention until he heard one of the boys talking about the man who was wearing an angry expression and an Illinois baseball cap. He froze where he was. Could it possibly be someone searching for them? There was no way to tell. Wearing an Illinois baseball cap wasn't exactly unusual. He was probably overreacting.

But what if he wasn't? Suddenly, he re-membered the men who had chased them down after Rick had been shot. The one man, the one called Jim, had worn an Illinois baseball cap. Tyler felt as though ice water was sliding through his veins. How would he have found them?

"Levi said he had a gun. I did not see it, but he looked mean enough to have one. Right?" The boy nodded at his friend.

The other boy, who had to be Levi, agreed. "*Jah.* It wasn't a hunting rifle, either. It was a gun like an *Englischer* would carry. Maybe a police officer. But I don't think that man was a police officer."

Neither did he.

His anxiety spiked. He needed to get his family out of there now. He walked around, searching for his wife and daughter, doing his best not to run. He didn't want to call attention to himself. Nor did he want anyone else to panic.

Abraham was ahead with William. He lengthened his stride to catch up with them. Putting his hands in his pockets, he walked beside them, trying to act as if he had not a care in the world. Inside, he was breaking apart at the seams.

"Abraham, would it be possible for us to leave soon?" he asked the other man quietly. His eyes darted to the side to make sure no one else had heard.

Abraham raised his eyebrows, but otherwise gave no other indication that it was an odd request. "I assume something happened?"

Although his manner remained calm, Tyler knew that was his cop voice. He'd heard similar tones from other cops he'd worked with. This was the first time that it was so personal, though.

"I heard a group of boys talking. There was a suspicious man in town with a gun. A man who may or may not be searching for us. The description, though, sounds a lot like a man who had chased us when we were traveling through Indiana. They don't know we are hiding here, and I know that I am probably overreacting. But I don't care. I want my family where I can see them."

Abraham rubbed his bearded chin. "I do not blame you in the least. I would want the same thing. Let's gather up our wives and the *kinner*, and we can leave in a few minutes. I need to let the bishop know what's happening."

Tyler winced. He understood completely. He was concerned, though, that the bishop might decide that the Everson—or rather the Miller—family was not worth the trouble. He would hate to be the reason any of these good people got hurt.

Within minutes, they were headed back to the farm. Kayla and Bethany were the only ones who talked on the way home. It was clear that the events had put a damper on the adults' moods.

Tyler constantly peered out of the buggy, expecting to see Jim or some other bully with a gun prowling along the streets. He didn't see anyone suspicious. That didn't relax his tension. He knew better that to let down his guard. These men were out there, and they were vicious.

The next morning, he stayed home and helped on the farm as much as he could. Abraham was going into town to grab some needed supplies. As he was getting the horse hitched up to the buggy, Tyler jogged out to him.

"Abraham, can you do me a favor while you're in town?"

"Maybe so," Abraham replied. Although he was not smiling, there was a definite twinkle in his eyes.

Tyler lowered his voice. "I want to see today's newspaper. There might be some mention of the man the boys saw in town. Hopefully, there will be information about him being arrested, but I want to see if there is anything useful."

"I can scan the paper for you," Abraham offered.

That was true. Tyler thought about it. "No. That's okay. I think I would feel better reading it myself. Sorry. I know you just bought one for us last week."

"I don't mind picking up another for you," Abraham replied.

When Abraham returned with the paper later that day, Tyler read through it. On page three, there was the mention that the police were looking for a suspicious man carrying a gun. It might have nothing to do with them.

Deep in his gut, Tyler couldn't quiet the feeling. Jim had somehow traced them to Ohio.

How long would it be until he found them?

FIFTEEN

What had she done?

Annie couldn't escape the feeling that disaster was pending. She prayed as hard as she knew how, but she still could not shake the dread that had taken hold of her. She replayed the conversation with her mother multiple times. Each time, she cringed. Why had she called her mother? Karl had called her back, and she had told him about the fire. He had assured her that her mother was fine.

Annabelle hadn't told him about the phone call.

She needed to tell Tyler what she had done. He'd be upset. And rightly so.

Hopefully, he would be better at the forgiveness thing than she had been.

She looked again at the newspaper. She had so many great memories at that house, but her mother was right. It was just a house. People were more important. That was why she had made that phone call.

"Annie?" She heard Julia calling.

"I'm coming," she answered.

Leaving the newspaper on the desk, she headed down the stairs. She was halfway down when she realized something. She had left her stockings off. It was a warm day, so her feet were not cold. It felt strange knowing that, for the first time in several years, she was not going to cover up her legs. Granted, no one in this house would care about the scars. But it still felt like a huge step for her.

Feeling lighter than she had in days, Annie waltzed into the kitchen. Julia was getting ready to leave. She had her stockings and her shoes on. She had also placed a black bonnet over her prayer *kapp*.

"I need to go out for a bit. I should be back within an hour. Will you be fine here by yourself?"

Annie nodded. "Of course! You go and run your errands. I will see you when you return."

She watched Julia as she headed out the door. It had been a while since she had been on her own. It was kind of nice.

Bethany found her a few minutes later. She had some books in her arms. "Mommy, will you read to me?"

"Of course I will."

Annie sat at the table with Bethany at her side. They read the first two books together. They had just opened the third book, when Annie looked up. She shuddered and the blood drained from her face. Jim, the man with the gun, was sneaking down the field toward the house. She could run, but what if he shot at Bethany?

She had to save her daughter.

How? With terror blazing through her veins, she realized that the only thing she could do was distract him.

"Bethy, I want you to listen to me." The little girl looked at her with wide eyes. "The bad man is coming. I can see him. I need to make you safe."

She hated the frightened expression that slid over her daughter's face, but she needed to make sure she understood the gravity of the situation. She needed Bethany to remain hidden until Tyler found her. Only then could she be sure that her daughter was safe.

Quickly, she brought Bethany into the pantry. It was hard to breathe around the terror that filled her system. Dragging Bethany over to the far wall, Annie pushed two shelving units apart just enough for her daughter to squeeze between them.

Helping her fit into the small space, she had her crouch down. "Okay, Bethany. I need you to stay here and not make a sound, do you understand?" She waited for her daughter to nod. "Good girl. Mommy is going to lead that bad man away from here so that he can't hurt you. Stay here and keep quiet."

Leaning forward, she kissed the blond head. She loved Bethany so much. She prayed that her daughter and Tyler would be safe. The question of whether or not she would ever see her daughter again popped into her mind, but she shoved it out. She couldn't give up. There was too much at stake.

As soon as she was sure her daughter was safe, she left the kitchen. She had not made it far into the house when a rough arm grabbed her and a calloused hand covered her mouth. The scent of old tobacco and sweat filled her nostrils. She gagged.

"Look who's here. I have searched for you and that sneaky husband of yours for weeks. I should have burned down your mama's house earlier. I would have had the reward money half spent by now." She cringed as a low chuckle filled her ears. Her call to her mother had led him right to them.

Jim forced her out of the house and down the street a short ways. There was a beat-up pickup truck parked along the side of the road. He grabbed some rope from inside and tied her hands. Then he forced her into the truck. He slammed the door behind her. "If you try to escape, somebody will die. And it will be your fault."

She believed him. Twenty seconds later, he hauled himself behind the wheel and started the truck. He didn't go far. He pulled the truck behind the empty house down the street and parked it. Then he took her inside. The house was falling down around them. The roof had holes in it. She could see the light from outside filtering through. The clouds were starting to gather up above. She had a feeling that the roof would leak like crazy once it started to pour. Then what?

Jim pushed her down onto the floor. She didn't want to look down to see what was covering the floor. It couldn't be good. She stared at Jim, waiting for him to tell her exactly what he planned.

He swung a decrepit chair around and sat facing her. The chair creaked.

"Your man, he's gonna be searching for you real soon. When he does, I'll catch him. I have a reward to get. Do you know how hard it was to figure out how to get it for myself? Kory was planning on getting his share. Tossing him off the bridge took care of that problem. I hadn't planned to kill him, but when I saw him almost fall through the bridge, I knew it would be easy to accomplish."

She had thought the other man had fallen. He had pushed him. The acid in her stomach churned.

"I decided that your mama would be the perfect lure, and I was right. I followed her to your brother's house. She likes to leave her phone in her unlocked car. I had a buddy put a bug in her cell phone, then I burned the house. I haven't had so much fun since I was kid. Always did like fire. When you called to check on your mother, we got to listen in. It took us a while to find you. But I was able to force someone at the cell phone company to look up her call records and where the calls came from. It was only a matter of time after that. We just had to talk to the right people to learn about a new family in the area."

Her phone call to her mother was going to cost Annie her life. And possibly Tyler's, too. Thankfully, she had been able to hide Bethany before Jim had gotten into the house. At least her little girl was safe. She couldn't believe how dumb she'd been. But she had been acting on pure nerve at that point.

The clip-clop of horse hooves made the foul man fall silent.

Jim stood and walked to the door. "Good, that other woman just pulled in the driveway. Soon, the whole crew should be home. When your man finds you gone, he'll come to find you. As soon as he's on his own, I'll make my move."

Jim gave a rusty chuckle and rubbed his hands together in glee.

"This is going to be so much fun," he gloated.

The dread that was roiling inside her went up a notch.

Where was Annie?

Tyler and Abraham had returned from helping the neighbor. Abraham immediately headed out to the barn to check on a project he'd set aside earlier. Tyler entered the house, but no one seemed to be there. Maybe she had gone somewhere with Julia. No, they wouldn't have left Kayla. Kayla was out in the front yard, playing by herself. That was odd. The girls had been each other's shadows ever since they had moved in with the Beiler family.

Maybe she knew where Bethany was. He

sauntered to the child and crouched down so that he was at eye level with her.

"Hi, Kayla. I was wondering if you knew where Bethany was. I need to find her."

Kayla blinked at him. "Nope. I looked for her. She wasn't inside." The seven-year-old shrugged her slim shoulders. In her world, not being able to find her friend one day didn't seem like a big deal.

Tyler had every reason to believe that it could be a very big deal. He jumped up and ran inside the house. Julia was baking something that smelled delicious in the kitchen. It barely registered with Tyler.

"Julia! Have you seen Bethany or Annie?"

She must have heard the fear threading through his voice. Stopping what she was doing, Julia shook her head. Her face paled slightly. She wiped her hands on a dish towel and started toward the door. "I'll check upstairs. I saw Annie about an hour ago, right before I left for town."

She ran lightly up the steps to Annie's room. He wasn't surprised when she came down a minute later. Her face was distressed. "She's not there. And there was no note or any sort of clue as to where she might have gone."

Julia's expression was becoming concerned.

Between the two of them, they searched the house for clues. Tyler was ready to scream. He heard a sniffling noise from the pantry. Walking in, he looked between two shelving units. Crouched down on the floor was Bethany, her face wet with tears.

Heart pounding, he pulled out his daughter and lifted her into his arms. He buried his face against the side of her *kapp* and held her tight. His baby girl was alive. He could not stop shaking.

Finally, he managed to walk out of the pantry, still holding her in his arms. Julia ran in and saw the child. She immediately wiped her eyes.

"Bethany," Tyler rasped out of a throat too tight. "Why were you in the pantry?"

The child gulped back another sob. "Mommy put me there. She told me to stay still and not move." A tear broke free. "I didn't move, Daddy. I didn't. I heard you calling, but Mommy said don't move."

His poor girl.

"Why did Mommy put you in there? Did she say?" His chest was tight. He knew that something horrible had happened. And he also knew that Annie had done all she could to protect the little girl.

"Mommy saw the bad man coming. She told me to stay so he wouldn't find me."

"This bad man," Julia said. "Did he come?"

Bethany nodded. "He made Mommy go with him. He said something about hurting Grandma if she didn't."

Of course Annie would do whatever she could to protect her mother. Really, to protect any of them.

Bethany started to cry again in earnest. "I want Mommy. Daddy, go find Mommy."

He kissed her, blinking back his own tears. "I will, bug. I'm gonna get Mommy as soon as I can."

He had no idea how. But he would find her. He went up to her room, to search and see if there was something that Julia might have missed. The room was spotless. The only thing out of place was a newspaper on the desk. He nearly walked by it without taking another look, but something about it made him glance down again.

The newspaper had obviously been handled a lot. It was wrinkled in various places and looked like it had been folded back to a specific page. The picture facing up was a burned-down house. At first, he almost missed it. Something about the picture caught his eye, though. When he looked closer, he realized that he knew the neighborhood. He had gone there frequently when he and Annie were still together.

It was his mother-in-law's house. All at once, he remembered how Annie had been on edge for the past week or so. Ever since he gave her the newspaper. He should have questioned her more. Maybe then she might have confided in him what had happened.

They had used her mother to draw them out.

He knew what he had to do. Searching the room quickly, he located the phone that Karl had given them. He dialed Karl's phone number, impatiently tapping his fingers on the table while he waited for it to be answered.

A deep voice answered. "Karl here."

"Karl. This is Tyler Everson." Tyler spit the words out so fast, he wasn't sure that the marshal would be able to understand him. He forced himself to slow down and speak at a normal rate. "I think that someone has taken my wife."

He quickly explained that Annie was missing. When he mentioned the newspaper opened on her desk to the article about the fire, Karl was concerned.

"She told me about the fire. My guess is

that she contacted her mother." Karl's voice didn't betray any judgment.

Tyler had already concluded the same thing. He also concluded that she had regretted her ill-advised actions. But it would have been too late. If only she had come to him. He would have helped her figure something out. At least, they should have called the marshals.

"I will send someone to check on the mother and brother. In the meantime, I will be there as soon as I can. If you hear from them, contact me at once."

Tyler agreed. The second he hung up, he headed outside. He was going to try and see if there were any hints outside. Bethany had said that Annie had seen the man coming. Tyler decided to walk the perimeter of the property, see if he could find any clues that might lead him to discover the whereabouts of his wife.

If she was still alive.

He had never in his life felt such despair. Reaching the barn, he looked inside and then around back. Nothing. Giving in, he let his knees buckle. Falling to the ground, he knelt on the fresh grass. And for the first time in his adult life, Tyler Everson truly poured out his anguish and his fears to God.

He had no idea how long he knelt there

behind the barn. When he finally stood, he felt renewed in purpose. He recalled a verse from his childhood. He thought it was from the Gospel of Matthew, but he wasn't sure. He didn't even remember the entire verse. The only part that he could recall was Jesus saying that He would be with them always. When all this was through, he was going to find a Bible and look up that verse.

Right now, he was going to find his wife.

He continued along the perimeter of the house. Abraham and William had joined in and were searching in another section of the property.

A drop of water hit him squarely on the cheek. Tyler glanced up at the sky. The clouds were dark and rolling through the sky at great speed. In the distance he saw a bright flash of light. Lightning. A few seconds later, thunder rumbled.

Great. He'd be searching in a thunderstorm.

He hoped that Annie was out of the elements.

He continued looking. He wanted to call out her name but restrained himself. She might hear him, but so might her kidnapper. He would lose any advantage he might have. Not that he had any. The kidnapper had to know that he was searching for her.

He kept going. Every now and then, he'd see a movement. It was always an animal or something blowing across the yard. He was trying not to lose hope.

Would he ever be able to tell her that he still loved her?

He hoped so. He needed to move faster. The rain was starting to fall harder. If it fell much harder, it would soon be hard to see anything more than a few inches in front of his face. His teeth chattered. The rain was cold. Within minutes, his clothing was soaked and his hair was plastered to his head. He shoved his hands in his pockets and kept his arms close to his body in an attempt to stay warm. He didn't even consider going back inside the house. Not while Annie was in the control of a madman with a gun. He said another quick prayer under his breath.

His ears strained. What was that? He listened. There it was again. There was a rustling sound. It was somewhere behind him. He started to pivot to locate the sound. Something hard was shoved into his back. He didn't have to look down to know that it was a gun.

He had been found.

SIXTEEN

Jim shoved the gun harder into Tyler's back.

"Don't try anything funny, you hear? I got your pretty little wife, and I have no problem with killing her to make you mind your manners."

Tyler did not doubt that the man would do just that. At least he knew that she was still alive. He allowed the man to push him away from the house toward the street. Every step would bring him closer to his wife. As they walked, he fought the urge to try and overpower the man forcing him along. He knew that there was a good chance that the gun would go off if he did. The other thought that kept running through his head was that this man was the only person who knew where Annie was.

The thunder boomed directly overhead. Lightning was now flashing in the sky with a vengeance, illuminating the surrounding landscape. It was frightening and awesome at the same time. The rain continued to pound on them. Soon the ground had turned into slippery mud. Tyler slipped once. The man behind him showed him no mercy. He smacked at Tyler with the gun. Tyler cringed, expecting the gun to go off. When it didn't, he straightened. Jim pushed at him again. They continued slogging through the summer storm until they reached their destination.

Jim pushed Tyler into the darkness of the falling-down house. Tyler had noticed the house in the past week or so. Abraham had told him that it had been standing deserted for two years now. There was no running electric. There was talk that the local government was going to tear down the building one of these days. It was a hazard and an eyesore.

Tyler heard someone ahead of him. His steps quickened. He was pretty sure that he would find Annie if he just kept moving. A light speared through the shadows. Jim had turned on a flashlight.

Sitting on the floor, her back against the wall, was his Annie. Her hands were tied in front of her. She looked uninjured. Momentarily forgetting the man walking behind him, Tyler skirted around the chair sitting in the middle of the floor and knelt down in the dirt beside his wife.

She was the most beautiful sight he had ever seen.

"Annie, are you hurt?" Was that hoarse croak his voice?

She stirred. Opening her eyes, she stared at him. "Tyler? Oh, Tyler." Her voice became a wail. "I am so sorry. I didn't mean to lead him to us."

"Hush, none of that. Remember what you keep trying to tell me? You are not responsible for someone else's bad choices. If I saw my mother's house had burned down, I would have called her, too."

"I didn't want you to come. I was hoping that you would be safe."

Another voice joined in, ruining their reunion. "Aw, ain't this sweet? I hate to interrupt this little party, but I have some business to take care of."

Jim stomped over to him and took out a pair of handcuffs. Who knew where he had gotten them. By the faint light of the flashlight, he ordered Tyler to put them on himself. He didn't dare argue, as the man was holding the gun aimed right at Annie's head.

At first, Tyler thought he meant to kill them right then and there. To Tyler's surprise, he merely walked over and sat down on the chair, keeping his gun trained on the pair of them. "As soon as this rain lets up, we'll be on our way. I will collect the money for killing you, make no mistake, but I am wondering if there is a way to make this whole business more profitable for myself."

Whatever the man was planning, Tyler wanted no part of it. He'd had a difficult afternoon. He was trying to keep his calm so that he could be cool-headed when the opportunity to escape and save Annie arose.

A clamor of voices outside caught his attention.

Abraham's voice was calling out his name. Annie's name.

The man holding the gun started muttering angrily. Tyler smiled in the darkness. He suddenly realized why the man hadn't just shot them. Any shots made would immediately lead people in this direction. The man didn't want to shoot them, then be forced to make a run for it without his proof that he had killed Tyler. He wouldn't be able to collect any money for that.

He could just take a picture with his phone. Tyler was a little amazed he hadn't done that yet.

Unless he planned to take them with him.

That seemed like it would be more hassle. Why would Jim want to haul two grown adults across the state with him if all he needed was proof that he had killed Tyler? The men's voices came closer. Tyler felt his hopes rise. Maybe the men would see their footprints in the mud. The hope faded as the voices continued past.

Jim laughed. Tyler felt Annie shudder beside him. He understood. That harsh bark was more of a bitter cough than a sound of humor.

He wished he could somehow comfort Annie. There was nothing he could do, though, except sit beside her in the dark and wait for the rain to stop. He still had one hope. Since Jim was waiting for the storm to break and light to return, they still had the chance that Karl or Abraham would arrive and intervene.

He held on to that hope for the next few hours. At some point, he must have drifted off to sleep. He awoke when someone kicked at his legs with steel-toed boots. The pain shot through his legs and into his hip. He didn't give the man the satisfaction of hearing him complain, though. Nor would he give up hope.

Karl and Abraham would keep looking for

them. They just had to hold out a little longer until they arrived.

The early morning light was starting to stream through the holes in the roof.

"We need to get out of here," Jim growled. "Before people start moving around. Stand up."

Tyler stood, then helped Annie to stand as best as could with the handcuffs on. She was moving stiffly this morning. Between her still-healing wound and sitting on the floor all night, it was no wonder.

He wished there was something he could do for her, but Jim wasn't a man of patience. As they left the building, Annie and Tyler went ahead of Jim, who kept his gun on them the entire time. He continued to push them to move faster.

Outside the building, the ground was slick with mud. Annie and Tyler both managed to sidestep the biggest patches.

Jim slipped. As he fell, the gun hit the ground and went off. Annie and Tyler both dove for the ground. Tyler heard a thunk as Annie hit her head on a rock. Jim scrambled to his feet, wild-eyed. He aimed the gun at Tyler.

Tyler took one look at the man and knew that he was going to shoot.

* * *

Annie felt Tyler's sudden stillness and forced herself to look up, blinking past the blinding pain in her head. Everything was blurry. After a few seconds, the blurriness faded enough for her to see the gun pointing straight at her husband.

"No!" she screamed.

A shot rang out.

Jim crumpled to the ground. Shouts and the sound of pounding feet headed their way. Arms gently lifted her. She saw that Tyler was on his feet, too.

Karl was there. His face was grim as he put a gun back into its holster. It made sense suddenly. Jim hadn't shot Tyler. It was the marshal's gun she had heard going off. The monster who had held her captive and had burned down her mother's house was dead.

The darkness was swirling around in her head.

She passed out.

When Annie woke again, she knew that she was in a hospital room. She could feel a bandage on her head. That was where she had hit her head on a rock. A doctor was leaning over her, flashing a light in her eyes.

She grimaced.

"Well, Mrs. Miller, I must say you are doing surprisingly well for someone who has been through your ordeal. I think you missed getting a concussion from that fall, although you did hit your head rather hard. You have five stitches in your head." He tapped the bandage on her left temple lightly.

Although she argued, the doctor insisted she remain overnight so that the staff could watch her for complications.

He came in to check her first thing the next morning. She wanted to dance when he said she could go home.

"Try to take it easy for the next few days, please," he cautioned, walking toward the door. "I am going to go write up some care instructions. Then you will be free to go."

She slumped back against the bed as he left. Five seconds after he left, the door opened again. She frowned until she saw who it was. Tyler walked in and her mood immediately picked up. He sauntered over to her bedside and kissed the tip of her nose.

"Come to spring me?"

He grinned, but she could see the shadows on his face. "Yes, ma'am. I am to bring you back to the house so that Julia may spoil you and Bethany can see that her mother is well."

Remembering what had started the awful

experience, Annie dropped her eyes in shame. "I betrayed you, Ty. I saw that picture of my mom's house, and I called her. I needed to hear her voice, but in doing so, I led him right to us." She explained how Jim had traced them. "Because of me, my mom was put in danger, and we were almost killed."

Tyler tipped up her chin with his finger. Reluctantly, she met his eyes. "Sweet Annie, it's not your fault. Who could blame you for wanting to check on your mom? I can't. I would have wanted to do the same."

She searched his eyes. He seemed sincere.

Her eyes widened. "We came in here dressed in our Amish clothes!"

He shook his head. "They made me change before I could enter. And they kept you covered up. No one was allowed to see you except the doctor and the marshals."

"And Karl? Is he kicking us out of the program?"

Even with Jim out of the way, she knew they weren't safe. Not while the trial was still in the future.

He sighed. "Karl's not happy. But he has decided to give us another chance. Especially since that Jim character is dead. He thinks that Jim died without telling others where we were. So for now, our cover is safe."

She closed her eyes briefly. When she opened them, she caught her breath at the intensity of his stare. "Don't—" he brought his head closer to hers "—ever do that to me again."

She knew he wasn't talking about the phone call. He was referring to her getting kidnapped and almost killed. After all that had happened between them, some feelings had remained. They might have even grown stronger. She really should keep her distance. Especially since they were both feeling so emotional after all that had happened.

Annie stayed where she was, anticipation zinging through her as her husband moved nearer. He was giving her a chance to back out, she realized. He was letting her make the choice.

Well, she'd already chosen. Looking at his face, she felt the emotion welling up inside her. The love that she had tried not to feel had grown back against her will. Only this time, the feelings were deeper, more mature than before. Knowing that danger was following them put a new perspective on things. She remembered Stacy's words to her and understood what the woman had been saying. Love was too precious to take for granted.

Annie finally admitted to herself that she loved Tyler.

Reaching up, she put her hand on the back of his neck and pulled his lips to hers. She caught his grin the moment before their lips touched. It had been three years since they had kissed. Now, as he gently pressed his lips against hers, she felt as if those years had never happened.

He lifted his head. Scanned her face. One of his hands stroked her head. Then he bent and kissed her again.

That evening, she went back to the Beiler home feeling optimistic, about her marriage, and about life in general. As the evening grew late, though, she could sense that Tyler was withdrawing into himself. And she couldn't understand why.

She went to bed, praying that it was all in her imagination.

Even though she knew it wasn't.

SEVENTEEN

He shouldn't have kissed her.

Tyler was still brooding about his poor judgment the following day. Tyler had seen the look in Annie's eyes. He knew that she was developing feelings for him again. Instead of filling him with joy, the notion filled him with dread. If she loved him, it would be difficult for her when they left witness protection and went their separate ways.

His heart ached to stay with her and Bethany. He knew that the love he had tried to deny feeling had just been dormant. Being with her, those feelings were coming to life again.

But they couldn't be together. The image of her lying in the hospital bed flashed through his mind. He squeezed his lids shut and clenched his teeth. He couldn't let that happen again. It was all his fault that she had been hurt. If he hadn't been so selfish and demanded that they stay together, she and Bethany might be somewhere on the other side of the country, safe and living their lives.

He knew that Annie was aware something was wrong. She'd been watching him for the past hour. When she'd tried to talk with him, the despair had bit deep into him. What he wouldn't give to be able to enjoy her company and tell her what was on his mind. He was done being selfish, though. As soon as he could, he had escaped to his room. Seeing that bandage on her forehead felt like an accusation. Every time he saw it, the guilt and fear cut deep into him.

He knew what he had to do. Remaining here was no longer an option. He would go. Once he was far enough away, he'd call Karl and plan to meet him. Karl could find him a separate placement.

It wouldn't be fair just to leave, though. He couldn't let her wonder what had happened to him. Going to the desk in his room, he pulled out some paper and sat to write a letter. His shoulders slumped. Shaking off his sorrow, he bent over the paper and wrote the hardest letter of his life.

Dear Annie,

I know that you are worried for me, and I am sorry for that. I can't stay and let my presence continue to endanger you and Bethany. I thought we could be a family. I was a fool.

As long as I am with you, then you are in danger.

I am leaving. Not because I don't care, but because I do.

I love you and Bethany with all my heart. I pray that you can forgive me. When she forgets me, can you remind Bethany about me? I know I have no right to ask, but I also know that your heart is too generous to deny this request.

Be well and be happy. With all my love, Tyler

Feeling like his heart had shattered in his chest, he quickly packed a bag and let himself out the window. His mouth twisted. It was a good thing his room was on the ground floor. Hefting his bag, he started off. Alone.

When Tyler didn't come out for lunch, Annie went to look for him. He had been acting strange all morning.

It was the kiss. He was regretting kissing her. She sighed. Tyler still felt overly responsible for their situation. She paused outside his door. It was time she told him she loved him and, just as important, that she forgave him. She had been carrying her anger and hurt around with her for so long, but it was time to let it go. It was time to reconcile with her husband.

Determined, she knocked on his door. He didn't answer. Acting on a hunch, she opened the door.

He wasn't there. Seeing the paper propped up on the desk with her name on it, she moved inside the room to get it, her feet feeling like they had cement blocks tied to them. She had a bad feeling about this.

Reading the letter, she felt the blood drain from her face. Shaking, she sank into the desk chair.

Oh, that stupid man! To go off and leave them without telling her, as if she didn't have a choice in the matter! She had loved him and lost him once because he decided to play the hero. She wasn't about to lose the man she loved a second time without fighting for their love and trying to save his life.

Clutching the letter in her hand, she ran out of the room and down the stairs. Bursting into the kitchen, she crashed to a stop in front of Abraham. Wordlessly, she handed him the letter. Honestly, she was so rattled she wasn't sure if she could speak right now. The anger at his high-handedness mingled with her very real fear for his life.

Abraham's face paled. "When did you last see him?"

"About an hour ago." She clasped her hands in front of her.

Abraham looked at his stepson. "William, go and look and see if any of the buggies or horses are missing."

Annie protested, "He wouldn't take any of your things."

"I know that, Annie. I need to check."

"Mommy?" Bethany's scared voice caught her attention. What did she tell her little girl?

"Bethany, sweetheart, eat your lunch and then I will take you and Kayla to the barn to see the kittens," Abraham announced.

Bethany brightened. She glanced at her mother before she agreed, though. Annabelle flicked a grateful look at Abraham. "That sounds like a great idea, Bethy!"

Satisfied, the child turned her attention back to her lunch.

Annabelle turned back to Abraham.

"I am going to get in touch with Karl."

She kept her voice low. "He needs to know about this." She rushed out of the room and back up the stairs. Once in her room, she rifled through her clothes until she found the cell phone that was buried there. It was a flip phone. The one she'd been given specifically to contact Karl if there was trouble.

Fumbling with the phone, she opened it and called the number that he had programmed into it. It rang once. Then it rang again. The anxiety in her mind spiked. When she got the voice mail, she hung up. Jonathan Mast. She would call him. Abraham gave her the number. The second ring was cut off abruptly. "Jonathan Mast speaking."

Annie wilted and sat on the bed. She felt too heavy for her legs to hold her up.

"Hello?"

"Jonathan, this is Annabelle, Annie Miller." Which name did she refer to herself as?

"Annie, yes. What's wrong?" His voice came back at once. The tears she'd been holding back spilled out of her eyes and rolled down her cheeks. A harsh sob welled up and burst out of her throat. It hurt. "Annie?" His voice was sharper.

"It—it's Tyler," she gasped out. "He's gone."

A pause.

"What do you mean he's gone? Where did he go?" Jonathan demanded.

"I don't know. He left me a letter. He blames himself for everything that has happened and went off. He wrote that he thinks Bethany and I would be safer without him here. I'm so scared. He's going to get himself killed."

"Annie, I want you to listen to me. I am on my way to you. I will be there as soon as I can. I am going to be calling the police near Harvest, and they will be searching for Tyler, too. If you hear from him, think of anything that will help us to find him, I want you to call me immediately. Do you understand?"

She nodded. Then grimaced at herself. "Yes. I understand."

The small click on the other end of the phone let her know that he had hung up. He was on his way. She caught her lip between her teeth. A sharp pain made her wince. She had bitten through the layer of skin. The metallic taste of blood hit her taste buds.

How long would it take him to get there? It all depended on where he was. It could be hours yet before he arrived. Hours in which Tyler could be caught and tortured. Or killed. And she was supposed to sit here while her husband was out there somewhere risking his neck? She knew why he had gone. He thought that if he left them, the marshals would continue to hide Annabelle and Bethany. No doubt they would get a totally new placement. Tyler, though, he seemed to believe that if he weren't with them, they would be safer. It was crazy thinking. They would be in danger no matter what as long as Barco was still a menace.

Tyler, however, seemed to be allowing his emotions to cloud his judgment. Like he'd done before. She should just let him go.

She could not do it. No matter how many times she told herself she was being foolish, Annabelle knew that she was going to have to go after her husband. No one else knew him like she did.

No one else loved him like she did.

And she had never even told him that she still loved him. She read his letter again. All the guilt, all the concern. No, she couldn't stay here while the husband she loved risked his life for her.

But she couldn't just leave. What about Bethany? Torn about what to do, she wavered.

Strengthening her resolve, she went downstairs and found Julia. "Julia, I need your help."

Julia fastened her concerned gaze on her new friend. "Anything. You know that."

She nodded. She felt guilty, because she was about to willfully deceive her friend. "Listen, Jonathan Mast is on his way. So are the police. They are all going to help find Tyler. Can you keep an eye on Bethany?"

She went back upstairs to change into her own clothes. She shoved the phone into the pocket of her jeans. As she was putting on her tennis shoes, her eyes fell on one of the scars that marred the smooth skin on her legs. Those scars had embarrassed her for so long. Why? She remembered Tyler's face when he touched the scar. The tenderness. The gentle care. She saw none of the disgust she had felt so often when she looked at them. Why? Because the scars did not—should not—define who she was as a person.

She was done hiding behind them.

A few minutes later, she was out the back door and going in search of her husband. She had no idea where she was going. But she remembered that Harvest had only one bus station. That seemed to be the most likely direction to go. Tyler was only an hour or so ahead of her. Hopefully, she could find him before he boarded a bus.

She walked for an hour. No sign of him. She started to pray. Every once in a while, her mind would wrangle with the notion that she might have taken the wrong road, or that she might have been headed in the wrong direction. If she had her own phone, it would have a GPS on it.

She shook the ideas away. She needed to keep going. She knew that she was going the right way.

A loud click on the left startled her. Spinning, she found herself staring into the face of a stranger. A handsome young man with a winsome face and a wealth of curly black hair. The man had a charming smile. He also had a gun, aimed right at her.

"Well, hello, Mrs. Everson," he said, almost pleasantly. "How nice of you to join me."

Tyler had left the house an hour and a half ago. He'd changed out of his Amish clothes and back into his own stuff and slipped out. He had walked for about an hour when he had come to his senses and realized that leaving his family would not make the danger go away. It would only cause three people pain. He turned back, intent on returning and begging his wife to take him back. He hadn't gotten far when he heard Annie's voice just around the bend. She must have found his letter almost immediately. And, in typical Annie style, she must have stormed out to find him.

Did she call the police? The marshals? He had no idea. When he had talked to Karl almost an hour ago, he didn't mention a call from Annie.

Karl hadn't been happy with his decision to leave. He felt bad, knowing the marshal was even now on his way to pick Tyler up. Hopefully, he wouldn't be too annoyed with him.

Strolling around the bend, he saw Annie struggling with a stranger. The man was doing his best to drag her along with him.

"Let her go!" Tyler yelled.

Annie gasped his name as he stepped forward. He glanced at her. Was she hurt? She didn't look hurt; she looked mad.

The man didn't let her go. Instead, he barked a harsh laugh. "Let her go? No way, man. I got a tip that you were seen down this road an hour ago. I never dreamed I would run into the missus here. She's my insurance that you will do exactly what I want."

He didn't protest when the man forced them to get into his truck. Tyler was at the wheel. Annie was in the middle, her leg touching his. The dark-haired man sat on the other side of Annie, his gun pressed into her side. Tyler had no doubt that if he made the wrong move, this man would casually pull the trigger and end his wife's life. Tyler had to think of a way to get her out.

It was clear in his mind that the smiling stranger had no intention of letting either of them live. Not after he'd let them both get such a clear image of him. Why hadn't he just shot them where they were? That was the question. Tyler knew that the bounty on him was for his death.

"I'm guessing you're wondering why you are still alive, aren't you?"

Tyler jerked. Having this savvy young man echo his thoughts was disconcerting, to say the least. "I know that you've figured out that I don't really have a use for you. But here's the thing. You have caused my family a lot of grief, Mr. Everson."

His family? Who was this kid? "My father is sitting in prison because you couldn't mind your own business. My mother, she's inconsolable."

"You're Barco's son." His voice was flat. Honestly, he couldn't even say he was surprised. Now that he thought of it, he could see the resemblance. Until that moment, he'd never seen Wilson Barco Jr.

"Obviously," the kid sneered. "I would have thought a lawyer would be smarter."

"So if you're not going to kill us—"

Annie's words broke off with a gasp. Tyler jerked his eyes around to see Junior pushing the gun harder into her side. Her face paled even more, gaining a waxy cast to it.

"Hey!" The truck swerved slightly as he reacted to the sight of his wife suffering at the man's hands.

"Careful!" Junior snarled. "You crash and she dies."

He straightened the truck, his knuckles going white as his grip on the steering wheel tightened. He had to keep his wits about him. As soon as he saw a chance to rescue Annie, he would take it. It no longer mattered what happened to him, as long as he could save her. And give her a chance to be returned safely to their daughter.

Junior was apparently only too happy to tell them all about his plans for them. "In answer to your question, Mrs. Everson, of course I'm going to kill you. I don't plan on letting someone else claim money that should go to me as my inheritance."

Charming. The family devotion boggled the mind.

"I think, however, that my mother would be comforted to know that you are suffering for what you have done to our family. The loss of business. You have no idea how much money has been lost because of you."

This was like a bad gangster show. He could hardly believe people actually thought this way. Except that this warped young man held a gun to Annie's side.

"How did you find us?" Annie asked.

"I've been keeping an eye on this situation. I know, for example, that your mother was used as bait. And that you bit and called her. When the man who burned down her house obtained records of your mom's phone calls, he told me about it. I think he thought I would up the bounty. It wasn't that hard to trace the phone you used. I was able to get a rough idea of where you were calling from. Flash your pictures around, and that's all it took."

Annie looked at Tyler out of the corner of her eye. He glanced down. Somehow the phone the marshals had given them was open on the seat beside him. She had called someone. Who? He sent up a prayer that the phone signal would be tracked.

He hoped it worked. Hoped someone found them, although it was unlikely.

One positive thought ran through his mind.

The man had no idea that they had been living with the Amish. That much was clear. He had no idea where to go to get to Bethany.

He drove for forty-five minutes, going through so many twists and turns that he could barely keep them straight in his mind. Every time they shifted, he checked the compass on the dashboard. The majority of the time, they were headed west. Back toward Chicago. Surely, they weren't going to drive this way for the next five hours, were they? Flicking his eyes to the gas gauge, he saw that they only had half a tank of gas left. Lifting his head, he had just enough time to see the police cruiser swerve in front of the truck. He turned the steering wheel and stomped his foot on the brake. The truck careened over to the side of the road, the right front tire going up over the embankment on the side of the road.

Wilson Barco Jr.'s head slammed against the passenger side window. He slumped, stunned. Tyler could hear the man breathe, so he knew that he wasn't dead. Who knew how long he'd been dazed, though.

Now was his chance. Yanking the gearshift, Tyler put the truck into Park. Then he threw open the door and jumped out, pulling Annie with him. She threw her legs over the side and made the small hop down before the two of them started to run, hand in hand, toward the police.

"Hey!"

Tyler turned and looked back. Barco's son was standing on the road taking aim. Tyler jerked Annie to his side and tried to hide her from Junior's view. A shot rang out. A burning pain seared into his shoulder. He didn't care.

"Keep running, Annie!" He followed her, waiting for the second shot. It went wide. The cops took aim, but they didn't fire. He and Annie were between them and Barco.

"Annie, get down," he told her.

The moment they were out of the way, the guns began to fire. He knew without looking that Barco was hit when they stopped. He wanted to look up, but found that his strength was gone.

"Tyler? Tyler! Get up!" He heard Annie's voice. It sounded like it was coming through a tunnel. It had an odd, echoing sound to it.

"Annie?" He couldn't make his mouth work right. His voice was muffled. He was going to pass out. His head was full of buzzing. The voices around him faded away.

When he came to, he was lying on his back. Annie was kneeling at his side. He'd never seen anything more beautiful than her pale face. Her brown eyes were flooded with tears. *Aww.* He hated that he had made her cry again. Actually, he hated that he had put her through everything she'd gone through in the past few weeks. When she'd asked if they could go into separate placements, he should have agreed. His gaze zeroed in on the bandage on her forehead. Another wound on his wife that he had to accept responsibility for. He regretted his selfishness.

How could he ask her to take him back after this?

"Ma'am, you need to move so we can treat him."

Annabelle's face was replaced by a paramedic's long face on one side. Jonathan Mast looked down on him from the other side.

"She was prettier." What was he saying? The paramedic rolled his eyes. Jonathan laughed quietly.

"I'm sure she was, Tyler. We have to get you to the hospital."

"Where—where's my daughter?" It was so hard to talk. He'd never felt so weak in his life.

"She's fine, Tyler," Annie said from the side. He moved his head back and forth, trying to crane his neck to see her. "Julia is watching her."

Julia. Exhausted, he sank back down, allowing the paramedic to care for him. He didn't protest when he was lifted gently onto the stretcher and placed in an ambulance. His eyes closed. He heard the door shut.

A warm hand took hold of his and held it. He pulled his lids open with an effort. Annie had come with him in the ambulance. His eyes devoured her face. "Are you all right?"

She smiled at him. It did funny things with his heart rhythm. "I'm fine, Tyler. You don't need to worry about me."

"Barco?"

Her smile dimmed slightly. "He didn't make it. He was killed at the scene. I told Jonathan what he had said about his mother. The marshals are going to check into whether or not she had any part in the illegal activities of her husband and son."

He certainly hoped not. "I hate that she has lost a son."

Annie sighed. "I do, too, but that is not your fault. Nor is it mine. The man made some really bad choices."

That was the truth. His eyes closed. He couldn't keep them open any longer. He let the darkness slide over him, knowing that Annie was beside him, holding his hand.

EIGHTEEN

Tyler hated hospitals. He couldn't step inside one without being reminded of Annie almost dying. Annie crying for him, in pain. Confused by the accident. That memory had haunted him for the past few years. Even though he was coming to terms with the fact that he wasn't completely to blame for what had happened, it still pained him to recall his beloved wife's suffering.

And yet here he was, lying in a hospital bed, a large bandage across his chest.

The memory of what had happened surged through him. His pulse spiked. Where were Annie and Bethany? His last memory was of Annie's face, pale and drawn with concern, as she leaned over him. But what if something had happened after he had blacked out? He couldn't just lie here! He had to go and find them, make sure they were safe!

Tyler struggled to sit up, desperate to discover what had become of his family. The stitches in his shoulder pulled. A slight twinge in his arm caught his attention. He looked down. For the first time since he woke up, he realized he was hooked up to an IV. A grimace twisted his face. He was a mess.

"Good afternoon, Ty. Glad you're awake."

His head jerked up. He hadn't even heard the door open. Jonathan Mast sauntered in. "Hey, Jonathan."

Jonathan stopped at the edge of his bed and narrowed his eyes. "You took quite a beating out there. I certainly hope you weren't planning on doing anything foolish. Like getting out of bed."

"I need to make sure that my wife is okay."

Jonathan reached out and placed a calming hand on his shoulder. The one without the stitches. "Relax. Annie is fine. Bethany is fine. Wilson Barco is still in jail. His son is dead. For now, the threat has been neutralized."

"For now." Tyler set his jaw. He had to do the right thing. No matter what it cost himself. "Look, Jonathan, I want you to find me a new placement."

The marshal's eyebrows moved closer together as he furrowed his forehead. "I can see why you would feel that way. You have to give me time to find a new placement. And to get the new identities together. And—"

"No." Tyler shook his head. Each word he said was like a chisel being hammered into his heart. "Not identities. Identity. I think that my girls would be safer if I wasn't with them."

The frown on Jonathan's face grew more pronounced. "Tyler, man, you don't want to do that. Do you? You know what it would mean. It could be years before it's safe for you to come out of the program. It's possible it may never be safe. If you go this route, then you will be separated from them. Maybe even for the rest of your life. I don't think you want to do that."

He didn't. Not even for a second. But it was the only way he could think of protecting them. "I do know that. But I also know that criminals like Barco are relentless. If I'm not around Annie and Bethany, maybe they would be easier to keep hidden. I will do whatever I need to do to keep them safe. Wouldn't you do whatever you could to protect the family you love?"

He could see that Jonathan was wrestling with the subject in his mind.

"Don't I get a say in all this?"

Annie. Tyler turned his head. His breath

caught in his throat at the lovely woman standing in the doorway. Her large brown eyes were shadowed. She had seen so much in the few weeks that they had been hidden with the Amish. He had never loved her more. It killed him to think of giving her up. She never took her eyes off him as she spoke to the marshal.

"Jonathan, may I please have a moment alone with my husband?"

The marshal hurried to the door. "Of course, Annie. Take your time." He was out of the room in a flash.

The silence stretched between them, awkward and tense with longing.

"I can't believe after all we've been through that you would even consider leaving us again. Tyler, I thought we could finally be a family. And now you're thinking of ripping us apart? Why?" She stepped up close to his side. If he wanted to, he could reach out and touch her. He curled his fingers into the bedsheet, controlling the impulse.

He sighed, wilting back against the pillow and closing his eyes briefly. When he opened them, she was still there, still staring at him with hurt on her face.

"Annie, we were building something. And for a short time, I actually thought it might work out. I love you, Annie. I never stopped loving you."

"Then why—"

He held up a hand. Not a command. A gentle plea. Surprisingly, she paused and waited for him to speak. "Annie, you know why I let you go the first time. I know you said there was nothing to forgive, that it wasn't my fault. But here we are in the same position again. My job has once again put you and Bethany in danger. If I leave, then maybe you could go on. Be safe and happy."

She was already shaking her head, a challenge in her flashing brown eyes. "You are not God, Tyler Everson. Even if you left, who is to say that these people wouldn't still come after us, to try and use us to bring you out? But even if no one ever tried to do that, Tyler, you can't let them decide how you live your life. All the bad decisions, those are things we can't help. And maybe you're right. Maybe we would be 'safer.'" Annabelle made air quotes with her fingers. "That doesn't mean we'd be happier. Tyler, I don't know how long we will have together. All I know is that I really do want to spend ''til death do us part' with you. With my husband. The husband I am choosing for a second time. And I want Bethany to have her father near as she grows up. And maybe a couple of brothers or sisters, in time."

He watched the color rise in her cheeks. How he loved this woman! And to think of raising a family with her, well, it would be his dearest wish. Would it be selfish?

"No, it wouldn't be selfish."

He blinked. He must have said that out loud.

"And you were wrong about another thing." Her words were soft, almost a whisper. "We might go on without you, but I don't feel like I could be happy. Not really. I would forever wonder where you were, if you were safe, if you were well. I wouldn't be able to stop myself. That's how this love thing works. Even if we try to convince ourselves we're fine, deep inside we're just lying to ourselves."

He already knew that. Hadn't he spent the past few years trying to keep busy just to fill the hollow void left by his family's absence? Could he even bear to go back to that lifestyle again, especially knowing she still loved him and had forgiven any wrong he'd done?

"I don't want to leave you," he admitted. "It breaks my heart to even contemplate taking that step. I would willingly give my life if it spared yours and Bethany's, though. You know that, right?"

She nodded, her eyes deep. They pulled him in. "And I feel the same. If you want to, we can ask Jonathan to relocate us. The whole family. I will move as many times as we need to. Just say we can stay together."

"Annie, it might mean that you can never see your mother again. Or Ethan."

"After what just happened I know very well that I cannot risk talking to my family until this is over. And I choose to believe that someday God will make the situation right."

Suddenly, it occurred to him that in all his planning, he had neglected the most important step. He hadn't prayed about it, hadn't involved God in his plans. Who was better equipped to keep his family safe than the Almighty?

"I think we should trust God with the whole problem. Just hand it over to Him." Annie's words hit him like a confirmation. How arrogant he'd been! Closing his eyes, he said a silent prayer, asking God to forgive him. *Lord, I put my family in Your hands, knowing they are far more capable than mine. Please protect us and teach us to follow Your will.*

Peace flooded his soul in a gentle wave.

The door swung open. Jonathan Mast re-entered the room. He looked between the two of them. "Okay, Tyler, here's the deal. I can move you to a different placement by yourself. But once I do, I can't change it. We have already made more changes than are normally allowed."

Feeling happier than he had since he woke up in the hospital, Tyler grinned. Jonathan looked taken aback by the expression. Annie's face tensed. He understood. He was, in essence, deciding his family's future. "About the new placement, Jonathan. I'm not going to be breaking up my family. We'll move together. We're in it together, until the end."

With a happy cry, Annie launched herself into his arms. He winced as her hand bounced off his wound. He didn't complain, though. Having her in his arms again was worth the pain. Over her head, Jonathan smiled at him and gave him a thumbs-up before he backed out of the room and closed the door softly behind him, leaving Tyler alone with his wife.

Annie raised her face, tears pooling in her eyes. One spilled over and streaked down her cheek. He caught it with his finger.

All at once, a look of horror crossed her face. "Oh! I forgot about your injury."

She started to pull away. He wouldn't let her go. "I'm fine. In fact, I'm more than fine."

His eyes searched her face. He tugged her closer.

"Tyler, I don't want to hurt you."

He traced a finger down her jaw. "A little pain I can deal with. What was really hurting was the idea of leaving you again." His finger paused as he searched her eyes. "I love you, Annie. Even more than I did when we got married."

Her face grew soft. "Oh, Tyler. I love you, too. I don't want us to be separated anymore."

He couldn't help the grin that spread across his face. "You know what I really need right now?" She shook her head. He lowered his voice. "I really need to kiss my wife."

She stilled, her face softening. "That can be arranged."

Annabelle shifted so that her face was close to his. He lifted his head and closed the remaining distance between them.

Annie stood in front of the sink, washing dishes. Her eyes searched the street every so often, watching for a car. Stacy had come to stay with them while the trial was going on. Karl had called her the night before to tell her that Tyler would be coming home the next day.

Annabelle couldn't wait to see her husband.

"Mommy, is Daddy here yet?"

Annabelle dried off her hands and faced her daughter. Bethany was carrying a large chicken. Rolling her eyes, Annabelle decided not to say anything, for now. When they had left the Harvest community, Bethany had missed Mrs. Feathers. Fortunately, their neighbors in their new community in Spartansburg, Pennsylvania, had plenty of chickens. They didn't care if Bethany carried one around.

"He'll be here today, honey. That's all I know."

The little girl sighed. "Me and Chicken are gonna go watch for him."

"I'll go with you," Stacy said. "We'll stay on the front porch since it's muddy from this morning's rain."

She placed her left hand on the child's shoulder. A gorgeous solitaire ring flashed in the light coming through the window. Annabelle was so happy for Karl and Stacy.

Jonathan had moved them almost immediately following their decision to stay together. For the most part, she was content. She was with her husband and her daughter. The only thing that made her sad was knowing that she would probably never see Julia and Abraham again. To keep them safe, Abraham and Julia had been moved to a new location, as well.

Annabelle shrugged off the momentary sadness. They were alive. They were together.

For now, she'd be good with that. They were living with a new Amish couple in a different community for the time being.

Her memories were interrupted by Bethany's squeal. "Daddy!"

Flinging the towel onto the counter, she ran out to the porch to greet Tyler and Karl.

Bethany and Annabelle both ran to be embraced by Tyler. The little family approached the porch together.

"Did the trial go well?"

Tyler nodded. "Yes. Barco was found guilty of all the charges against him. He's not going to be getting out of prison, probably for the rest of his life."

"And," Karl said, "we were able to seize his assets. Which means the bounty is no more."

Annabelle's heart stopped. "Does that mean—"

"We can go home." Tyler hugged her tight.

She hugged him back. They would go home. Together.

EPILOGUE

"The ceremony was lovely, Annabelle."

Annabelle turned and smiled as her friend and neighbor, Danielle Johnson, moved to stand beside her. Danielle had saved her life when she'd called Annabelle three months earlier to warn her that someone had been watching her house. Annabelle's heart was full, seeing her friend here to celebrate with them.

She allowed her gaze to wander across the lawn. The trees were vibrant with changing hues of red, orange and gold. She loved autumn. Bursts of color were everywhere you looked. The air even had a different smell to it, fresh and crisp. It was her favorite season. And now it was even more special. Today was Tyler and Annabelle's eighth anniversary. To celebrate, they had decided to bring their friends and family together so they could renew their vows to show their renewed commitment to each other.

Danielle's husband, Mike, and Tyler were standing near the barbecue grill, deep in conversation. Maybe Tyler was telling Mike about his new job. Annabelle sighed, content. Tyler had given up criminal law altogether. He now worked in an up-and-coming firm that specialized in family law. And even better, after today, he would be moving in with Annabelle and Bethany.

Stacy and Karl were talking to her brother, Ethan. They were holding hands.

Jonathan Mast and his wife, Celeste, joined them. Rick was with them. Tears stung her eyes—she was grateful that he had recovered so well.

Laughter drew her attention back to the group. Celeste was laughing at something Jonathan was saying to their daughter. Celeste seemed to be one of those women who took to motherhood naturally. And their new daughter was precious. She'd slept through the entire ceremony, cozy and warm in her mother's arms. As she watched, Jonathan reached out and took his daughter from Celeste's arms. The look of love on his face as he looked down at his baby girl made her sigh.

Her eyes sought out Tyler. When she found

him, a sigh of content left her. He winked at her, the warm look in his eyes bringing a flush to her cheeks.

"Uh-oh." Danielle gave her a pointed look. "You guys are so cute, the way you keep watching each other."

She shook her head but couldn't stop smiling. "I thought what we had was dead. To find love again with him, it's been amazing."

"You look happy," Danielle stated.

"I am happy." Annabelle shielded her eyes against the glare of the sun with her right hand. "I'm amazed at how close Tyler and I have grown. I loved him when we first got married, but now, the feelings are even stronger. More intense. It's almost like we are different people." She shook her head. "I can't explain it."

"Aren't you different people, though?" Danielle cocked her eyebrow at Annabelle. "God is part of your relationship now. And I think, going through what you guys have just survived, it really made you look at what was important."

That made sense. A commotion out on the lawn distracted her. Both women turned as shouts and giggled erupted.

Laughter bubbled up inside Annabelle and spilled forth as three very wound-up little girls chased each other around the lawn, followed by a small puppy, who was happily yipping as she played. Annabelle's brother had gifted them with the black Labrador soon after they returned home for good. He claimed that nothing said stability and home like a dog. Bethany had taken one look at the dog and it was instant love.

Annabelle hadn't wanted a dog just yet. Even Tyler had been doubtful. Until Bethany had handed the squirming puppy to her father. Annabelle had watched, amused and resigned, as he immediately melted and announced that they needed a good name for her.

"You know that she just manipulated you, right?" Annabelle had told him. "You're wrapped around her finger and she knows it."

Tyler had just shrugged with a smile. "I don't care. I won't let it go too far. But I am just so glad to have you both back in my life."

So was she.

Annabelle raised her left hand and took a sip of the Pepsi she was holding. The sunlight glinted off the rings on her hand. She couldn't help but marvel at how blessed she had been.

Her mother had hosted the reception that followed the simple ceremony where Tyler and Annabelle had renewed their wedding vows.

"This has been a beautiful day, hasn't it?" She closed her eyes and lifted her chin, enjoying the cool breeze that played with her hair. She'd left it down today, the way that Tyler liked it. She enjoyed the feeling of the sun on her bare head. Although, sometimes she missed the simplicity of the life they'd experienced briefly when they were living with the Amish.

"Not as beautiful as my new-old wife," a warm voice whispered in her ear. She shivered.

Tyler. Her smile edged into a grin. He wrapped his arms around her from behind and pulled her back against him. She sighed as she leaned back into him. Gratitude for the love they had rediscovered filled her. She could barely speak through all the emotions whirling inside her.

"Walk with me?" Tyler asked, rubbing his chin against the top of her head.

"Anywhere."

Holding hands, they wandered amid their guests, talking and laughing. Every once in a while, Annabelle squeezed Tyler's hand, just for the pleasure of feeling him squeeze back in response. A few times, he raised their joined hands so that he could place a kiss on her knuckles. She sighed when he did. And she noticed that some of the other women did the same.

Sorry, ladies. He was all hers.

"You good?" He leaned down to whisper in her ear. The love she saw in his blue-gray eyes sent a thrill trickling down her spine. She was so blessed that they had found each other again.

"I'm fine," she whispered back. "Just feeling emotional."

"I meant it, you know."

She quirked an eyebrow at him, confused. "Meant what?"

"I love you and our daughter more than anything. I won't let myself be blinded again."

Turning slightly, Annabelle raised her free hand to gently cup his cheek. The soft whiskers of his beard, now neatly trimmed up, tickled her palm. "I know that. I was just thanking God for giving us another chance. I love you so much."

The intensity of his eyes deepened. The world shrank to the two of them. When he leaned forward to kiss her, she rose up on her toes to meet him halfway.

The crowd around them burst into applause. She jerked back, startled.

Tyler laughed and pulled her close again. "They'll have to get used to it," he said before capturing her lips again. Annabelle melted into the kiss, smiling against her husband's lips.

* * * * *

Dear Reader,

I hope you enjoyed Annabelle and Tyler's story, the conclusion of the Amish Witness Protection miniseries. I had so much fun writing this story. I especially enjoyed the challenge of writing with other authors. It was fun trying to make sure that names, descriptions and key characters were consistent.

One of my favorite aspects of this story was how Tyler and Annabelle were willing to overcome their fears for each other and their daughter, Bethany. Even very real fears like the fear of heights were no match for the love of family.

Thank you for joining me on this journey.

I love to connect with readers. You can contact me through my website, www.danarlynn. com. Feel free to sign up for my newsletter, too! Or you can follow me on social media.

Blessings,
Dana R. Lynn

Get 4 FREE REWARDS!

We'll send you 2 FREE Books <u>plus</u> 2 FREE Mystery Gifts.

Love Inspired® books feature contemporary inspirational romances with Christian characters facing the challenges of life and love.

FREE
Value Over
$20

YES! Please send me 2 FREE Love Inspired® Romance novels and my 2 FREE mystery gifts (gifts are worth about $10 retail). After receiving them, if I don't wish to receive any more books, I can return the shipping statement marked "cancel." If I don't cancel, I will receive 6 brand-new novels every month and be billed just $5.24 for the regular-print edition or $5.74 each for the larger-print edition in the U.S., or $5.74 each for the regular-print edition or $6.24 each for the larger-print edition in Canada. That's a savings of at least 13% off the cover price. It's quite a bargain! Shipping and handling is just 50¢ per book in the U.S. and 75¢ per book in Canada.* I understand that accepting the 2 free books and gifts places me under no obligation to buy anything. I can always return a shipment and cancel at any time. The free books and gifts are mine to keep no matter what I decide.

Choose one: ☐ **Love Inspired® Romance**
Regular-Print
(105/305 IDN GMY4)

☐ **Love Inspired® Romance**
Larger-Print
(122/322 IDN GMY4)

Name (please print)

Address   Apt. #

City   State/Province   Zip/Postal Code

Mail to the **Reader Service:**
IN U.S.A.: P.O. Box 1341, Buffalo, NY 14240-8531
IN CANADA: P.O. Box 603, Fort Erie, Ontario L2A 5X3

Want to try 2 free books from another series? Call 1-800-873-8635 or visit www.ReaderService.com.

---

*Terms and prices subject to change without notice. Prices do not include sales taxes, which will be charged (if applicable) based on your state or country of residence. Canadian residents will be charged applicable taxes. Offer not valid in Quebec. This offer is limited to one order per household. Books received may not be as shown. Not valid for current subscribers to Love Inspired Romance books. All orders subject to approval. Credit or debit balances in a customer's account(s) may be offset by any other outstanding balance owed by or to the customer. Please allow 4 to 6 weeks for delivery. Offer available while quantities last.

Your Privacy—The Reader Service is committed to protecting your privacy. Our Privacy Policy is available online at www.ReaderService.com or upon request from the Reader Service. We make a portion of our mailing list available to reputable third parties that offer products we believe may interest you. If you prefer that we not exchange your name with third parties, or if you wish to clarify or modify your communication preferences, please visit us at www.ReaderService.com/consumerschoice or write to us at Reader Service Preference Service, P.O. Box 9062, Buffalo, NY 14240-9062. Include your complete name and address.

LI19R

Their Family Legacy
Lorraine Beatty

The Rancher's Answered Prayer
Arlene James

Get 4 FREE REWARDS!

We'll send you 2 FREE Books
<u>plus</u> 2 FREE Mystery Gifts.

Harlequin® Heartwarming™ Larger-Print books feature traditional values of home, family, community and—most of all—love.

FREE
Value Over
$20

YES! Please send me 2 FREE Harlequin® Heartwarming™ Larger-Print novels and my 2 FREE mystery gifts (gifts worth about $10 retail). After receiving them, if I don't wish to receive any more books, I can return the shipping statement marked "cancel." If I don't cancel, I will receive 4 brand-new larger-print novels every month and be billed just $5.49 per book in the U.S. or $6.24 per book in Canada. That's a savings of at least 19% off the cover price. It's quite a bargain! Shipping and handling is just 50¢ per book in the U.S. and 75¢ per book in Canada.* I understand that accepting the 2 free books and gifts places me under no obligation to buy anything. I can always return a shipment and cancel at any time. The free books and gifts are mine to keep no matter what I decide.

161/361 IDN GMY3

Name (please print)

Address   Apt. #

City   State/Province   Zip/Postal Code

Mail to the **Reader Service:**
IN U.S.A.: P.O. Box 1341, Buffalo, NY 14240-8531
IN CANADA: P.O. Box 603, Fort Erie, Ontario L2A 5X3

Want to try 2 free books from another series! Call 1-800-873-8635 or visit www.ReaderService.com.

MUST ♥ DOGS COLLECTION

SAVE 30% AND GET A FREE GIFT!

Finding true love can be "ruff"— but not when adorable dogs help to play matchmaker in these inspiring romantic "tails."

YES! Please send me the first shipment of four books from the **Must ♥ Dogs Collection**. If I don't cancel, I will continue to receive four books a month for two additional months, and I will be billed at the same discount price of $18.20 U.S./$20.30 CAN., plus $1.99 for shipping and handling.* That's a 30% discount off the cover prices! Plus, I'll receive a FREE adorable, hand-painted dog figurine in every shipment (approx. retail value of $4.99)! I am under no obligation to purchase anything and I may cancel at any time by marking "cancel" on the shipping statement and returning the shipment. I may keep the FREE books no matter what I decide.

☐ 256 HCN 4331   ☐ 456 HCN 4331

Name (please print)

Address   Apt. #

City   State/Province   Zip/Postal Code

Mail to the **Reader Service:**
IN U.S.A.: P.O. Box 1867, Buffalo, NY. 14240-1867
IN CANADA: P.O. Box 609, Fort Erie, Ontario L2A 5X3

READERSERVICE.COM

Manage your account online!

- Review your order history
- Manage your payments
- Update your address

> *We've designed the*
> *Reader Service website*
> *just for you.*

Enjoy all the features!

- Discover new series available to you, and read excerpts from any series.
- Respond to mailings and special monthly offers.
- Browse the Bonus Bucks catalog and online-only exclusives.
- Share your feedback.

Visit us at:
ReaderService.com

RS16R